The Lighthouse
Berkley Street Series Book 2
Written by Ron Ripley
Edited by Emma Salam and Lance Piao

ISBN: 9781537155371
Copyright © 2016 by ScareStreet.com

Thank You and Bonus Novel!

I'd like to take a moment to thank you for your ongoing support. You make this all possible! To really show you my appreciation for purchasing this book, **I'd love to send you a full-length horror novel in 3 formats (MOBI, EPUB and PDF) absolutely free!**

Download your full-length horror novel, get free short stories, and receive future discounts by visiting www.ScareStreet.com/RonRipley

See you in the shadows,
Ron Ripley

Chapter 1: Squirrel Island

The dawn was breathtakingly beautiful, and for that Mike Puller was extremely thankful. The strong, powerful scent of the Atlantic was heavy in his nose as the waves pounded against the boulders of Squirrel Island. Behind him, the Lighthouse stood tall and majestic. The keeper's house, which was painted the same stark white as the lighthouse, was empty.

Waiting. Mike thought, shuddering. *Waiting for me.*

He reached his hand into the breast pocket of his work shirt and removed the letter he had written. The short note was tucked into an envelope, which in turn was sealed in a pair of Ziploc sandwich bags.

For a moment, Mike held the letter, the plastic cool and thin beneath his fingers. Finally, he sighed, put the letter on the pier beside him, and put a large stone on the bag. The light gray of the rock contrasted sharply with the dark wood of the pier. The construction was new, not yet weathered by Atlantic storms or the Nor'easters which come down from Canada. A light wind came in from the east, but not enough to do more than flutter the loose edge of the sandwich bag.

Mike got to his feet and quickly undressed. The early June air was surprisingly warm. He folded each item of clothing as he took it off and soon he had a neat, tidy pile beside the gray stone.

He climbed down from the pier, stepped onto a large boulder, and then strode into the piercing cold of the ocean. Instantly he shivered, his body attempting to rebel against the sudden change of temperature. His flesh seemed to crawl and pucker simultaneously. At first, his legs refused to move, his hands gripping at the stones. Each and every muscle urged him to step back towards the lighthouse. Self-preservation screamed at him to get out of the Atlantic.

Mike ignored it, and overrode the need to live.

He couldn't stay on Squirrel Island.

No, Mike thought, stepping further out. *She made that perfectly clear.*

His foot slipped, and he plunged down into a crevice. For a moment, he struggled to free himself, the surface of the water only inches from his head. A wave rolled in, pushed him back, and Mike relaxed.

It's easy, he told himself.

Michael Patrick Puller opened his mouth and inhaled.

Chapter 2: Going for a Ride

Marie Lafontaine held on tightly to the side of the boat.

Jesus, am I going to be sick? she wondered.

Amy glanced over at her and asked, "You doing alright, Marie?"

Marie hesitated, then nodded. "You didn't say the waves were going to be this rough."

Amy shook her head, grinning. "This is called a 'calm sea,' my friend. You should see it when it's rough."

"There's a reason why I live in a city, Amy," Marie said, trying to keep focused on the lighthouse which drew rapidly nearer. "So, what made you decide to purchase a lighthouse?"

"I bought the island," Amy said. "I wanted a little peace and quiet plus the price couldn't be beat."

"How much did you pay?" Marie asked.

"A dollar," Amy answered smugly.

"What?"

"One United States dollar," Amy said.

"Wow," Marie said.

"Not really," Amy replied. "The Squirrel Island lighthouse is on the national registry of historic buildings."

"What does that mean?"

"It means," Amy said, "there are certain things I can do and certain things I cannot. Also, part of the purchase contract requires me to bring the lighthouse up to code, maintain it, and ensure its survival."

"Oh," Marie responded.

Amy nodded, guiding the boat toward the pier which extended from the island. "I hired a contractor to live out here for the first couple of weeks. He and I both agreed it would be easier for him to do the repairs that way. I haven't heard from him in a few days, and I want to make sure he hasn't taken off with all of the supplies and equipment. Plus, I wanted to show my cousin the lighthouse.

"You know," Amy said, glancing at her and winking, "do a little bit of the whole, look at what I've got and you don't."

"Real nice," Marie said, shaking her head. "I thought we were done with one-upping each other in high school."

"No, not at all," Amy said with a laugh. "You might have been, but I wasn't."

"So this is your way of saying you've won because you've got the most stuff?" Marie asked.

"Exactly," Amy said sweetly.

"Thanks," Marie said, grinning. "You're such a good cousin. I'm happy you've got your own little island, literally, but I wish it wasn't so far from the shore. Or have to ride in a boat to get there."

"Stay put," Amy said, laughing. "Let me get the boat secured."

Marie watched, impressed as Amy brought the small vessel in, side-bumping against the pier gently.

"Amy," Marie said, straightening up. "Are those clothes?"

Her cousin looked away from the pier's edge. "Yeah. That's strange."

The clothing was folded neatly, stacked beside a bowling ball sized stone. A plastic bag of some sort was under the rock.

Suicide, Marie thought instantly. She had seen how suicide victims often left their clothes. Orderly piles. One last effort from a confused mind to organize something and make sense of some small part of the world.

"Amy," Marie said.

The tone of Marie's voice caused Amy's eyes to widen in surprise. "What?"

"Once you get this boat tied up, I want you to stay in it, okay?" Marie asked.

"Why?"

"Please," Marie said, "this is the cop talking now. Something bad has happened here, and I don't want you to be the first one to see it."

Amy nodded. She threw a loop of thick rope around a piling, pulled the slipknot tight and turned the engine off completely. With the absence of the diesel's rumbling, the sound of the Atlantic filled Marie's ears. Her queasy stomach was forgotten as she grabbed hold of the pier and climbed out of the boat.

Her legs quivered for a moment, her head spun, and she slowly looked up and down the length of the pier. On the island, the lighthouse stood tall. A small house, which was attached to it, had closed shutters over the windows and a faded blue door.

Marie walked to the pile of clothing and squatted down.

Work boots, Marie thought. *Blue jeans. Socks. Boxer briefs. T-shirt. Sweatshirt. Note.*

She reached out, carefully tilted the stone back and slipped the Ziploc bag out from under it. There were two bags, and then an envelope.

'Ms. Amy Kahlil.'

"Marie," Amy called. "What's going on?"

"Hold on," Marie said. She opened the bags, slipped out the envelope and broke the seal on it. Inside was a single piece of white notebook paper.

> *Dear Ms. Amy,*
> *I'm sorry. She doesn't want me here. She won't let me stay. I have to leave. She won't let me call. She won't let me stay.*
> *She won't let me stay.*
> *Mike Puller*

Marie put the letter back in the envelope and stood up. She looked around the pier and then stopped. A flash of white caught her eye, and she turned to the left. A wave rolled in, slapped the stones loudly, white foam breaking apart. She stepped closer to the edge and peered down.

Only a few inches beneath the surface of the water was a body. His arms were outspread, and he was naked and covered in thousands of minute crabs. The creatures crawled over him, pulled off tiny pieces of flesh and devoured them, fighting one another as they did so.

Marie's stomach churned, and she closed her eyes. She had regained her composure before she called out, "Amy."

"Yeah?"

"Call 911, please," Marie said, opening her eyes and turning away from the body.

"Why?" Amy asked, a hint of panic in her voice. "What's wrong?"

"Your handyman killed himself," Marie said bluntly, walking over to her cousin.

Amy's eyes widened, and her face paled. "I can't call," Amy whispered. "Mike and I communicated through emails; for some reason, there's no cell reception out here."

Marie frowned. "Alright. Head back to shore, get a hold of the police. Tell them there's been a suicide and that I'm here. Make sure you tell them I'm a detective with the Nashua police department. Got it?"

Amy nodded. "Should we do anything?"

"Nothing to do," Marie said.

"Shouldn't you come back with me?" Amy asked. "I mean, if he's dead, why do you have to stay here?"

"Because I don't want anyone else to show up," Marie replied. "We don't need someone to decide they want a look at the lighthouse and find a body. Okay?"

"Yeah," Amy said. "Okay."

Marie watched her cousin get the boat ready to go, and then she waved goodbye as Amy backed the boat out and headed back towards the shore.

Once Amy was gone, Marie walked up the pier to a small patch of overgrown grass in front of the closed-up house. There was a fresh lock on the door, and the shutters as well. She walked around the house and found a pile of boards of various sizes beneath a tarp. The windows on the back of the house were shuttered and locked. A tall brick chimney rose up, and a large amount of seasoned firewood was neatly stacked.

A dull-gray metal bulkhead was beside the chimney, and this, too, was secured shut.

It's like he was trying to keep something or someone from escaping, Marie thought.

She moved on to the lighthouse and found that its door, painted the same as the house's, was also locked tight. On the far side of the lighthouse, she found a single-person tent. In front of it was a fire pit, a cooler off to the right. A rustling sound came from the interior of the tent and for a moment Marie's breath caught in her throat. Cautiously she bent down, took hold of the loose flap and pulled it back.

A middle-aged woman sat in the semi-darkness. She wore a plain, soft blue dress. Her hands were neatly folded in her lap, and her salt and pepper hair was pulled back into a loose bun. Her features were fine, gently rounded with age. Crow's feet spread out from the corners of her light gray eyes as her full lips parted in a smile. Her teeth were slightly yellowed, and a little crooked.

The edges of the woman were fuzzy, and even in the dimness of the tent Marie could almost make out the back fabric of the interior straight through her.

She's a ghost, Marie thought with cold certainty. The hair on her neck stood on end, and her back was rigid with fear.

"He left," the woman said.

"He did," Marie managed to say.

"You should too."

The woman vanished, and Marie let the tent flap fall noiselessly back into place.

Trust me, Marie thought, hurrying back to the pier. *I'll be leaving here just as soon as I can.*

She sat down by Mike Puller's clothes, avoided the crabs and their feast, and waited impatiently for Amy to return.

Chapter 3: A Surprise Guest

Shane Ryan sat on his back steps and lit his first cigarette of the day. It wasn't enjoyable, and it wasn't refreshing, but it definitely took the edge off the morning.

Which is the whole point of the thing, Shane told himself. He tapped the ashes off into an ashtray, took a drink of coffee and enjoyed the warmth of the sun on his face.

"Shane," Carl said.

He turned his face to the left and saw his dead friend. In German, he said, "Good morning, Carl."

"Good morning to you, my young friend," Carl replied in the same language. "You have a guest."

Shane took a pull off of the cigarette, looked at Carl warily and asked, "Alive or dead?"

"Alive," Carl answered. "It is your friend, the policewoman."

"Marie?" Shane asked. He picked up his coffee and stood up. "At six in the morning?"

"Yes," Carl said. "She should be ringing the bell in a moment."

The grand old doorbell of the house chimed as Shane stepped into the kitchen. He put the cigarette out in an old coffee can by the sink and hurried out to the main hall and the front door.

When he opened it, Marie was standing on the doorstep.

"Come on in," he said, stepping aside. "You pick the most ungodly hour to come calling, you know."

"I know," Marie said, smiling at him as she entered the house. "I also know you get up early."

"Very true," Shane said. He closed the front door, saying, "Come on into the study."

They entered the room and once Marie had sat down in one of the club chairs, he did the same.

"Everything okay?" he asked.

She opened her mouth, hesitated, then said, "I have a favor to ask."

"Sure," Shane said. "What do you need?"

In quick, short sentences, with the words seeming to tumble out one on top of the other, she told him about the Squirrel Island Lighthouse, a suicide, and a ghost.

"My cousin's really upset," Marie said. "I mean, I'm not too happy about seeing the crabs feasting on a corpse, but she's invested in this place. She can't have a malicious spirit haunting it."

She can, Shane wanted to say, but he kept the thought to himself. "Agreed. Now tell me, Marie, what would you like me to do about it?"

"I was thinking about how you got rid of your ghost here," Marie said. "I was hoping you'd be able to do the same at the lighthouse."

Shane sat back in his chair, frowning. He reached up, rubbed the back of his head and said, "It's not as easy as that."

"I didn't think it would be," she replied, "but I thought if anyone could do it, it would be you."

He smiled. "I appreciate the confidence, I do. I think the only way I could help is if I actually went to the island and stayed in the lighthouse for a while."

"What would that do?" Marie asked.

"Let me get to know the woman there," Shane said, his smile fading. "Once I get to know her, maybe get a grip on who she is, I might be able to make her leave. I can't guarantee it, though."

"I know," Marie said. "But I'd be happy as hell if you'd try."

"For you," he said gently, "I'd be more than willing to try."

She blushed slightly, reminding him again of how she was more than a detective. Once more his heart ached at the memory of what they almost had.

Marie's blush faded, and she smiled. "When do you think you could go?"

"If you want to hang around for about half an hour, forty-five minutes tops," Shane said, "I can get everything I need. I mean, there is internet service, right?"

"Yeah," Marie said, nodding. "It's strange. There's a booster on a new solar array in the lighthouse, and it helps with getting a direct satellite connection, but there's no cell reception."

"We can keep in touch through email," Shane said, getting to his feet. "I'll bring my laptop and the essentials."

Marie stood up and smiled at him. "Thank you, Shane."

She gave him a strong, fierce hug, and he returned it happily.

"You want to wait down here?" he asked. "Or up in the library?"

Marie shook her head, stepping out of his embrace. "No. Not me. Your ghosts still scare the hell out of me."

"Me too, sometimes," Shane said seriously. "Alright, I'll see you in the car then."

"I'll grab some food from Jeannotte's Corner Store, do you want anything?" Marie asked.

"A carton of Lucky Strikes," Shane said, "and a box of matches. Everything else I need is here."

"You need to quit smoking," she said as she left the room.

"Yeah," Shane agreed, following her out. "Later."

She shook her head and made her way to the front door. Shane turned and went up the stairs. He had to pack.

Chapter 4: A Meeting with Amy

Shane had never been a fan of the ocean. Or water, in particular. Not since the house and the girl in the duck pond.

He had smoked half a pack of cigarettes as he and Marie sat at a picnic table in a rest area. Amy was on her way, according to Marie.

The sooner, the better, Shane thought. He looked out over the Atlantic, and in the clear, bright sunlight of the morning, he could see the lighthouse. It was small from where they sat, and the idea of being on an island in the middle of the ocean turned his stomach.

He took out a cigarette, lit it off the one he was finishing, and sighed.

Marie glanced at him. "You okay?"

He shrugged. "Don't particularly care for water."

"Why?" she asked.

"Aside from the dead girl in the pond," Shane said, "I don't like the idea of being a lower member of the food chain."

"What?" Marie asked, confused.

"Sharks," Shane said. "I don't want to be eaten by a shark."

She laughed, saying, "Shane, there aren't any sharks here."

"Yes, there are," Shane said, exhaling a long stream of smoke. "Listen, there are constant sightings of great whites off the coast of Massachusetts, and the damned things come up here, too."

Marie shook her head. "Shane, you're not going to get eaten by sharks."

"Not if I stay out of the water," he agreed.

She rolled her eyes, then turned her attention to the entrance of the rest stop as a large, black Cadillac SUV pulled in. The driver, hidden by the vehicle's tinted windows, shut off the engine and then opened the door.

A woman who looked to be roughly Marie's age got out and waved.

Marie returned the wave and stood up. Shane did the same, examining the driver.

She was tall and lithe, dressed in a flower print summer dress. Her skin was a delicate tan as if she spent the perfect amount of time in the sun and not a second more. She walked delicately, yet with a commanding presence. She was a confident person, and Shane heard it as soon as she spoke.

"Amy," Marie said happily, embracing her.

"Hey Marie," Amy said, grinning. "And you're Shane?"

"I am," Shane said, offering his hand.

She shook it, her grip strong. "You're going to help me with this problem of mine?"

"I'll do what I can," Shane responded.

"I do appreciate it," Amy said. "Do you want to talk here, or somewhere else?"

"Here, if we could," Shane said. "If you don't mind. Not too many places allow you to smoke inside anymore."

"So long as I'm upwind, I don't mind at all," Amy said, smiling.

They all sat down at the table, and Shane looked expectantly to Amy.

"Okay," she said, brushing a lock of light brown hair behind her ear. "I'm sure my cousin has given you the basics of what happened the other day?"

Shane nodded.

"Right," Amy said. "Good. I did a little digging in the town library, and over in the historical society. Turns out the lighthouse has a bad reputation. Suicides. Murders. People vanishing."

"For how long?" Shane asked.

"Ever since the first stones were laid for the foundation," Amy said, frowning. "And let me tell you, all of the rumors have come back in full force since Mike's unfortunate death."

"What do you mean?" Marie said.

"I went to hire another couple of contractors," Amy explained. "Told them what I wanted, and they were all gung-ho and ready to work until someone who was nearby asked if it was for the Squirrel Island lighthouse. When I told them that it was, one of the contractors asked if the rumors about Mike Puller's incident were true. Again, I said it was. And that was that. Word has spread like wildfire, and I can't find anyone from Pepperell, Massachusetts to Kennebunk Port, Maine who'll do the work for me."

"That bad?" Shane asked.

Amy nodded. "A few of them said that as soon as the place was cleared of its bad luck, they'd be happy to come do the work for me."

Marie snorted derisively. "They won't even work in teams?"

"No," Amy said, shaking her head. "I offered that too. Even wanted to bring an exorcist, but the guys said it wouldn't do."

"It won't," Shane said.

The two women looked at him.

He lit a fresh cigarette and sighed. "Exorcisms do pretty much one of two things. They either send some poor lost soul out into the big bad world, which is just as bad for them as it is for us, or they make a mad ghost even madder."

"Oh," Amy said, surprised.

Shane nodded.

"What's your suggestion?" Amy asked.

"Let me stay on the island for a while," Shane said. "I'll figure out what's going on. Then, well, we'll see what happens. I might be able to convince the spirit there to leave."

"Really?" Amy said. "Are you serious?"

"Yes," Shane said. "But remember, I said 'might.' I'm not guaranteeing anything."

"Do you want money for this?" Amy asked.

"No," Shane said. "Just make sure I have food and come out if I ask you to. I do my work remotely, so I should be good there. I've got a carton of cigarettes. Two-fifths of whiskey, and the complete works of Raymond Chandler. I'll be good for a little while."

"If you're sure," Amy said, "I can bring you out there right now. You coming for the ride, Marie?"

"Hell no," Marie said decisively. "I don't like boats, and the last trip hasn't changed my mind."

Shane grinned and said, "Alright, then. Let's get my gear out of your car and into Amy's."

They stood up from the picnic table, and Shane looked out once more at the lighthouse.

How bad could it actually be? he wondered. He shook his head, took a final drag off the cigarette and stubbed it out.

Chapter 5: Squirrel Island Lighthouse

Shane was alone.

Amy had given him a quick tour, helped him put his belongings in the keeper's house, and then was on her way back to the mainland.

Shane had an itch at the base of his skull, as though someone was staring at the back of his head.

Someone probably is, he thought. He walked down to the edge of the island and strolled along the perimeter. In the distance, he could make out sails and people out in their small boats and yachts. A ferry made its way from some island to the next and Shane shook his head. He enjoyed the beauty of the ocean. The power which lay beneath the waves.

But he was respectful of it as well. He'd been aboard ships on training missions, and had seen deep-sea storms throw destroyers and battleships around like bath toys. While a rogue wave wasn't likely, he knew full well how one could rip everything on Squirrel Island out into the depths.

Let's not get too morose, he chided himself.

When he reached the pier, he followed the old path from the water's edge up to the keeper's house. He had already taken the locks off of the doors and windows, thrown open the shutters and set up his belongings.

There hadn't been much to it.

He had a sleeping bag, his pack of cigarettes, whiskey, books, and laptop. A change of clothes were kept in his pack. Canned food and bottled water had been stocked up for the unfortunate Mike Puller, and they were still there for Shane.

Whose future fortunes have yet to be decided, Shane thought, grinning. He went in, sat down on his sleeping bag and looked at the afternoon light as it played across the interior of the room.

Where he was making his camp had once been the living room for the keeper and his family. Off of it was a kitchen, a small stairwell leading to a loft bedroom, and a small office. The house was barren of furniture. The cabinet doors had long been removed from the kitchen's cabinets, and the dull white walls were a maze of cracks. The stairs leading up looked iffy at best, and Shane wasn't certain he wanted to go into the cellar without a shotgun.

The whole place felt *off*.

He reached over, grabbed his pack and pulled it to him. He rifled around in it, pushed aside a sweatshirt and smiled. He brought out his iron knuckles, the deadly weapon which had served him so well in Rye and Mont Vernon.

He slipped them on and nodded to himself. *Play it safe. Play it smart.*

Sighing, Shane settled back against the wall, closed his eyes, and relaxed as best he could. Sooner rather than later, it would be night, and he suspected the island would be far more active then.

The soft creak of an unoiled hinge woke Shane up from a fitful sleep.

Beyond the windows, he could see the night sky and the wide-reaching arc of the lighthouse's beam. He heard a soft whir followed by a click as the lantern above completed its rotation.

Yeah, Shane thought, sitting up. *That sound could get old real quick.*

He reached over, found his pack, and pulled out the camp light he had purchased on the way up to the shore. With a flick of a switch, light burst out and filled the room.

Damn! he thought, setting the lantern down clumsily and rubbing at his eyes. White spots exploded behind his eyelids. *Stupid. Way to blow your night vision.*

After a minute, Shane dropped his hands, blinked, and looked around the room. It was eerie, frightening in a new way. The walls seemed to breathe; the house felt like a living entity around him.

Shane shook his head, picked up his water bottle, and had a long drink of the warm liquid. When he finished, he wiped his mouth with the back of his hand, sighed and thought, *Suppose it's time to get another look at the place.*

Shane got to his feet and stopped.

The floor above him creaked. Footsteps crossed the loft and paused at the top of the stairs. Shane took a deep breath and turned to face them. As he did so, the unknown intruder descended the stairs. Each step creaked, squealed beneath some weight. Soon, the visitor reached the bottom and stood, unseen, in what was the former living room.

Shane waited.

"Who are you?" a woman asked. Her voice was cold, brutal and unforgiving.

"My name's Shane," he replied. "May I ask yours?"

She didn't answer. She didn't walk away either.

"I've been asked to speak with you," Shane said.

Still, she remained silent for a few more moments.

"I am Dorothy," she said finally. "And you are not welcome. None of you are. Leave, or I will make you go."

Her footsteps went up the stairs, across the floor, and silence fell over the house again.

Great, Shane thought. *I'm not welcome. This should make it a hell of a lot more difficult.*

Chapter 6: Drunk at Sea

Dane, Scott, Courtney, and Eileen all relaxed comfortably in Scott's father's yacht. All of them were more than a little drunk, and it took Scott quite a while to realize they that had lost their anchor and were drifting along with the current. The understanding of their situation helped to take the edge off his inebriated state.

At twenty-two, Scott was not a sailor nor had he ever been. He had always been far more interested in the young ladies that a yacht attracted rather than the yacht itself. Scott didn't have any of the necessary licenses to operate a yacht or even a boating license.

Oh my God, Scott thought, getting shakily to his feet. *I am absolutely screwed.*

He looked out at the expanse of the Atlantic and tried to see something, anything which looked like the shore. Running aground would be terrible, especially since his father had quite expressively forbidden Scott from even *thinking* about the yacht, let alone taking it out.

Better to beach the damned thing than sink it, Scott thought. Gripping the handrail he made his way to where Dane lay with his thick arm wrapped around Eileen's equally thick waist.

"Dane," Scott said, nudging his friend with the toe of his boat shoe. "Dane!"

Dane opened one eye, which rolled drunkenly until it focused on Scott. Dane grinned and slurred, "What's up?"

"We're screwed!" Scott snapped. "That's what's up."

"Not yet," Dane argued, closing his eye. "Too much whiskey."

Scott pushed Dane roughly. "Don't pass out!"

Dane opened both eyes and sat up a little. "What're you being such a pain about?"

"The anchor's gone!" Scott hissed.

"Bull," Dane said, struggling to look around. "We're fine."

Dane got up, glanced around, stopped, turned his attention to the sails, and said softly, "Jesus, Scott."

Scott helped his friend to his feet, steadied him as best he could, and together they stood at the rail. A wide beam of light passed over them, moved in a wide arc to the left, vanished, and then reappeared.

"Holy Christ," Dane said.

"What?" Scott asked. "What's wrong?"

"That's the Squirrel Island lighthouse," Dane said. "We're miles from where we should be, Scott. And if we don't get in on the lee side of the island, the breeze'll run us straight out and up along the Maine coast."

"What do we do, now?" Scott asked, feeling panic creep into his voice.

Dane tried to turn towards the wheel, stumbled, caught himself, and sank to his knees. He stuck his head between the upper and lower bars of the rail and vomited straight into the Atlantic. Again and again, Dane threw up, until Scott, feeling sick from the sight and smell of the bile, turned away. Finally, when Dane had finished dry-heaving, Scott helped him up.

"There's a pier, on the island," Dane managed to say as they reached the wheel. "You need to drop the sails while I steer, can you do that?"

"I think so," Scott said. "But why?"

"We'll run aground if we don't take the sails in and get the engine started," Dane replied. "Wake Eileen up, she knows a little about sailing. Tell her we need an emergency anchor. Then wake Courtney up, have her fire up the engine."

"We can't just beach the yacht?" Scott asked.

Dane's expression was one of horror. "There's no place to beach her, Scott. Squirrel Island is nothing but rock, and I don't know this area. I don't know where the shoals are, or where anything is along this stretch of beach. She won't beach. She'll break up, and if we don't pull our act together, we're going down with her."

Fear, it seemed, had burned all traces of the alcohol out of Dane's system.

Scott managed to wake both of the girls up. Soon, they were all frantically—if somewhat drunkenly—getting the yacht ready. The sails came down, Eileen managed to fashion an anchor from a length of the line and a small, spare anchor found below deck, and Courtney got the engine running.

With the motor powering the yacht, Dane guided it in close to Squirrel Island, and when they were a short distance away, he yelled out to Eileen. Eileen gave a thumbs up, and heaved the anchor overboard. Seconds later, the anchor struck bottom and the yacht, *A Father's Dream*, came to a gentle stop as Courtney cut the engine.

The anchor line went taut, then slackened as the yacht floated easily at anchor.

Scott sank down to the deck and let out a long sigh. *Thank God he's away for the weekend,* Scott thought, imagining what his father's reaction might be if he ever learned of the debacle. He shuddered at the idea of how angry his father would be. The man had never struck Scott, but Scott believed that could quickly change.

Dane and the girls came over to him.

"Unbelievable," Courtney said, her face flush with excitement. "That was great!"

Scott raised an eyebrow. "I would definitely not describe it as 'great.' Or anything other than terrible. It's not your father's yacht, sweetheart."

She stuck out her tongue and sat down across from him.

"Hey, isn't the lighthouse supposed to be automated?" Eileen asked.

"I don't know," Scott replied sulkily. His head was starting to hurt.

"It is," Dane answered. "There aren't any more manned lighthouses. At least not on the East Coast."

"Then, why is there a light on in the house over there?" she said, pointing out at the island.

"I don't know," Dane answered softly.

Scott twisted around, saw light streaming out of a window. His stomach rumbled. "Wonder if they have any food."

Courtney said, "Right! I'm starving."

Dane shook his head. "No. I'm not going ashore. I'd rather stay right here. I don't trust anyone squatting on an island. Something's not right."

"God, Dane," Eileen said, looking at him. "You are such an old lady sometimes."

"Do you guys not watch the news?" Dane asked.

"About what?" Scott said, laughing. "Crazies living on islands where they can't even get cable? Get over it, Dane."

Scott pulled himself up and stood, holding onto the rail. A wave of sickness flooded him, but he waited a moment, and it passed as quickly as it had arrived. "Come on. Let's get the jolly boat down and over to the pier."

"You know," Courtney said, "I heard somebody actually bought the place. I bet they're working on it out here."

"Where's their boat, then?" Dane asked grumpily. "How the hell are they getting back and forth to the island? And why would they stay the night?"

"They probably just left a light on, you big baby," Eileen said, laughing. She walked over to the jolly boat and said, "Come on, let's get this in the water."

Scott and Courtney went to help her and after a short, sullen silence, Dane did as well.

Soon, the four of them were crowded into the small jolly boat with Scott on the oars. It took less than five minutes to row to the pier, but it was enough to drench Scott in sweat and put an ache in his arms. He was more than happy to ship the oars, and he watched as Dane secured the boat to the pier and then helped each of them up and onto it.

When the four of them stood together, they looked up to the lighthouse and the keeper's house. Both of them were a soft, gentle white in the darkness of the night. The barest hint of a path led from the end of the pier to the front door of the keeper's house. The light in the window was bright, yet not nearly as powerful as the beam sent out by the lighthouse's lantern.

"Ready?" Eileen asked.

Scott and the others assented as she started up the path, the rest following her confident lead. A cool wind set a chill into Scott's flesh, and he realized the June night was unseasonably cold. He shivered, suddenly conscious of the light clothing he was wearing.

Christ, I hope it's warm in there, Scott thought.

The walk was blessedly short, if slightly uphill, and they came to a stop before the door. Eileen boldly knocked on it.

"Who is it?" a man demanded from the house, his voice coming through the door and out of the window.

"My name's Eileen," she said loudly. "My friends and I are in a jam. Our yacht is at anchor a little off the island, and we're hungry. We only planned for a day trip, and something happened. We can't get into the harbor until morning. We don't know the coast around here and, well, we didn't plan for anything really."

The lock slid back, and the door opened. An older man, perhaps in his forties, stood in the doorway. He was bald and lean, his skin pale. He wore only a pair of shorts, and was in good shape. On his right breast, he had a large tattoo: the eagle, globe and anchor of the United States Marine Corps. On his left breast, in spiderlike script, he had the words *Until Valhalla.*

The man studied them in an awkward silence, then stepped to one side, saying, "Come on in."

They all said thank you, and walked into the room.

It was of a decent size, with a door on the back wall, and another on the right. A set of narrow stairs led to a second floor. The room was in rough shape, the plaster on the walls looking as if it would come tumbling down at any moment. The only light was a Coleman camping lantern. On the floor was a sleeping bag, a backpack, and a laptop, along with some other odds and ends. The man, evidently, was not expecting company.

Their host closed the door, but he didn't lock it.

"My name's Shane," he said. "Take a seat. I've got some food in the kitchen. Not much, but it should be enough to quiet your stomachs until you leave in the morning."

"Anything would be great," Courtney said.

Shane nodded and left the room. He returned a minute later with an armful of bottled waters and a box of packaged peanut-butter crackers. Quietly, he handed them out, kept a package of crackers for himself along with a bottle of water and sat down on his sleeping bag.

Scott ate the food quickly and drank the water the same way. The fear of losing his father's yacht had made him ravenous.

Shortly, when the food was gone, Dane said, "Shane, why are you here?"

Shane took a drink of water, capped the bottle and put it down beside him before he answered. "I'm here because of some ghosts."

"Really?" Courtney asked excitedly. "Like, real ghosts? Is the place haunted?"

Shane nodded. "Yeah. It's haunted. You may all want to get back to your yacht before the dead take notice of you."

Scott snorted. "What are they going to do, scare us and keep us awake all night?"

Shane smiled at him politely. "No. They may, however, convince you to commit suicide, or outright kill you. Keeping you awake really isn't on their bucket list."

Everyone chuckled, then the humor faded as they realized Shane was serious.

"You're joking?" Dane asked.

Shane shook his head. "Not about this. Some ghosts aren't exactly pleasant or generous. Some aren't misunderstood or unable to move on because of some horrible personal tragedy." Shane's voice was cold and hard.

"Some simply like to hurt people," he continued. "Some of them refuse to accept death and instead, begin to punish those around them. Whatever the reasons for this place's dead, they don't matter right now. What does matter is all of you getting out of here and being safe. I can't give you much more; I don't expect to be resupplied for another couple of days, and I really don't like to be hungry."

Dane scoffed. Eileen closed her eyes and snuggled up against him.

Scott looked at the bald man. *I don't know if I believe him or not.*

Courtney looked at Shane and said, "The ghost here. Is he bad?"

"She," Shane corrected gently. "It's a 'she.' And I do believe she is. I'm here because she convinced the contractor hired to fix the place to drown himself. No one's going to be able to live here if she keeps doing that."

"I heard about that," Scott said. "What I heard, though, is that he went for a swim and got caught in the rocks and drowned."

"Well, what actually happened," Shane said coldly, "is she harassed him to the point where he killed himself."

"How?" Courtney asked. "How can someone talk someone else into suicide?"

"Lots of ways," Shane said softly. "Sleep deprivation. Fear. Isolation. All of those factors are here. Suicide, he believed, was the only way he could escape her."

"How do you know that?" Dane asked.

"He left a note," Shane replied.

"There was no mention of a note in the news," Courtney said. "Why wouldn't they say there was a note?"

Shane shrugged. "I'm sure it sounded crazy. And who wants to have their loved one's madness splashed all over the evening news?"

"So," Dane said, "who's the ghost?"

"Her name's Dorothy," Shane answered. "I don't think she likes me."

"Could she hurt you?" Eileen asked.

"She'll definitely try," Shane said. "She might succeed, too. Ghosts can cause a hell of a lot of damage when they want to. Even kill you if they've got enough power."

Scott shook his head, Dane laughed, and Eileen grumbled as she adjusted herself in the young man's embrace. Courtney glared at Dane.

"This isn't funny, Dane," Courtney said angrily.

"Oh come on!" Dane said, chuckling. "You don't believe this crap, do you? I mean, seriously? Ghosts? And they can hurt you, too? That's absolute bull, Cort, and you know it."

Shane gave Dane a hard, angry look. Then, in a low voice, thick with disdain he said, "I don't care what you do or don't believe. But you're in here as a courtesy. Keep running your mouth and you can leave. Be respectful. You don't have to agree. Just be polite."

The cold, harsh tone of the man forced a nod out of Dane.

"We should get back to the yacht anyway," Scott said. He stood up, stretched and added, "Thanks for the food and water, though."

Shane nodded.

Scott looked out the window as the others stood up and he whispered, "What the hell?"

Chapter 7: A Painful Realization

"What?" Dane asked. "What's wrong?"

"The jolly boat's gone," Scott said.

Dane got to his feet. "Where the hell did it go?"

Eileen looked up at Dane and asked, "Didn't you secure it?"

"Of course, I did!" Dane snapped, anger dancing in his eyes. He turned to face Shane and said, "Alright, who else is on the island, and why in God's name would they steal the boat?"

"Oh no," Scott said softly, cutting off any reply Shane might have been readying. On the pier stood a naked man, and Scott could see the yacht through the man.

Dane choked back something, took half a step backwards and fell onto the floor. Both of the girls scrambled to their feet, crowding around Scott at the window.

"Why is he naked?" Eileen asked.

"Yeah, oh Jesus," Courtney gasped. To Shane, she said, "Why can we see through him?"

Shane picked up his water bottle, drank some and then said, "Because he's dead."

Courtney sat down, her back against the wall so she could face the bald man. Scott joined her, and Eileen did the same as Dane got into a sitting position. Courtney asked, "Who is he?"

"If he's naked and at the pier," Shane said, "then, more than likely, he's the contractor who committed suicide last week. Mike Puller, I think that was his name."

"Why is he here?" Courtney asked.

Shane shrugged. "Depends on the person. Depends on the place, too. If this woman is as strong as she seems, then she has bound him here. Possibly others as well. I'll find out soon enough, I guess."

"How are we supposed to get to the yacht?" Dane asked, his voice small.

"Is there a second boat?" Shane asked.

"No," Scott answered. "Just the one."

"We can call for help, right?" Eileen said, looking around as she dug her phone out of a pocket.

"It won't work," Shane said. "No reception here."

"I always have reception," Eileen said. She frowned. "This can't be right. I don't have any reception. None!"

"She doesn't want us to use phones," Shane said. He picked up his laptop, tried to power it up and shook his head. "Great. Nothing on mine now."

Scott checked his phone, as Courtney and Dane did the same.

Absolute zero, Scott sighed. His phone wasn't even turning on.

"Damn it!" Eileen said, dropping her phone to her lap. "It just died!"

"If they're all dead," Shane said, "it means she's draining them."

"What?" Dane asked, confused.

"There's a theory that ghosts are energy," Shane explained, "and they can drain the charge out of a battery to give themselves extra strength."

"Great," Eileen muttered.

"Could we swim to the yacht?" Scott asked Dane.

Dane shook his head. "No. Not this close to an island. We wouldn't be able to get through the surf, and if we did, there's no accounting for the currents around us. I'm a decent swimmer, Scott, and even I wouldn't risk it."

"Is someone coming here for you?" Eileen asked Shane.

"Couple of days," Shane replied. "Sooner, I hope, when I don't contact them tomorrow morning."

"This is insane," Scott said. "We can't be trapped on an island."

"We can," Shane disagreed. "And it seems like we are."

"What are we going to do about food?" Courtney asked.

"I brought enough for myself for a week," Shane said. "If we ration it we can stretch it between the five of us for a couple of days. We may need to make it last for three, but I hope not. I hate being hungry."

Silence filled the small room, broken only by the steady click of the lighthouse's lantern.

"Why is it so cold?" Courtney asked.

"You don't want to know," Shane said. He stood up. "There's wood out back, I'll bring some in and get a fire going. It'll fight off the chill, and give us a little peace of mind."

Scott watched the older man go through the doorway in the back wall, then an unseen door was opened. The others looked at Scott, and Scott shrugged.

The place felt vile, and the situation seemed even worse.

Chapter 8: The Dawn Arrives

Shane sat on the front step of the keeper's house. He was dressed, smoking a cigarette and finishing the last of his morning whiskey.

"Good morning," a young woman said.

Shane twisted around and saw Courtney, who had her black hair cut in a pixie style. She was exceptionally pale, her eyes large and green. She was short, perhaps no more than five feet tall and lithe, Shane realized, was the best way to describe her.

"Good morning," Shane said. He moved over to the right and patted the stone beside him. "Take a seat. Need a cigarette?"

"No, thanks," she answered, sitting down beside him. She smelled of the ocean and sweat, alcohol and fear.

"Whiskey?"

Courtney's eyes widened a hair, and she laughed. It was a good, rich sound which made Shane smile. "No. Thank you, though. You always drink whiskey first thing in the morning?"

"Breakfast of champions," Shane said, getting out another cigarette and lighting it. He exhaled and added, "I have terrible nightmares. Absolutely foul. Whiskey is the only thing that takes the edge off."

"I'm sorry to hear that," Courtney said.

Shane grinned. "No worries. I'm essentially a functioning alcoholic."

"Do you have alopecia?" Courtney asked suddenly.

"I do," Shane said, surprised. "Don't meet too many people who know about it. They either figure I'm a diseased freak or a freak who Nairs all of his body hair."

Courtney chuckled. "No. My younger sister has it. Not as serious as you, though; patches here and there on her head."

"I'm sure it's rougher on women," Shane said. "Men can usually get away with being bald. Society still can't turn away from a woman who has a bald head, either by choice or by nature's design."

"She's lucky," Courtney said. "Our mom has figured out how to comb and pin her hair so Andrea isn't made fun of."

"How old is your sister?" Shane asked.

"Twelve."

"How are you even old enough to drink, if you have a twelve-year-old sister?" Shane asked.

Courtney blushed slightly. "I'm twenty-six, but I look younger than I am."

"You look good," Shane said, taking a long drag off of his cigarette.

Her blush deepened.

"Scott doesn't tell you that nearly enough, I'm sure," Shane said.

She raised an eyebrow.

Shane grinned. "Common fault among men. Especially when they're between the ages of thirteen and forty-two."

Courtney laughed. "And how old are you?"

"Forty-three," Shane replied. "Old enough to know better, dumb enough to forget every so often."

"Well," Courtney said, "I'm willing to listen whenever you want to say it."

Shane let out a pleased laugh, nodded, and said, "Sounds like a deal to me."

A pleasant silence wrapped around them and the Atlantic went about its ageless motions. A short distance away, the yacht bobbed at her anchor, a reminder of how the four travelers were trapped with him.

"Shane," Courtney said.

"Yeah?"

"How did you get involved in this? I mean, why are you here?" she asked.

"It's a long story," Shane said. "But, if you want to hear it, let me get some coffee going on the stove, and we can sit in the kitchen, and I can tell you my long, sad story."

Chapter 9: Miserable

When Scott woke up on the hard floor of the keeper's house on Squirrel Island, he instantly knew the previous night had not been a bad dream.

Oh, Christ Almighty, he thought miserably, *Dad is going to kill me. Straight up murder me, bring me out to the middle of the Atlantic, and dump my body. Just as soon as he gets another boat.*

He got up slowly, his body aching from the poor and painful sleep of the night before, and stretched. The smell of fresh coffee widened his eyes a little, and he stepped over Dane and Eileen. Both of whom snored loudly as they spooned. Scott went into the kitchen, and he saw Shane had a fire going on the small wood stove. Shane sat with Courtney, the two of them sharing a cup of coffee.

A spike of jealousy drove through the morning haze of Scott's brain and the emotion burned violently as Shane gestured to him.

"Come on in, Scott," the older man said. "Take a seat. Sorry about the lack of hygiene here, but I have only the one cup."

Courtney took a last drink, passed the tin mug to Shane, and Shane got up and went to the stove. He used a t-shirt to take the bluestone percolator off the iron heating plate and poured the dark, rich liquid.

The smell was phenomenal and went a long way towards easing Scott's jealousy.

"Take a seat," Shane said, passing the cup to Scott. "And I'm sorry, but I don't have any sugar or cream. Don't use the stuff myself."

"I think it'll be alright this morning," Scott replied, sitting down between Courtney and Shane.

The older man, who was wearing a pair of blue jeans and a black tee shirt, rummaged in a box on the countertop. He pulled out a bulky, brown plastic bag of some sort and handed it to Scott.

Scott accepted it with his free hand, read the label on the package and said, "What's an 'MRE?'"

Shane grinned and leaned against the counter. "In theory, it is a

'Meal Ready to Enjoy.' The newer generations, they aren't half bad. The ones I first ate when I joined the service, well, those were of dubious culinary delight."

"This says vegetarian lasagna," Scott said. "So, it's a dinner?"

"It is a fifteen hundred calorie meal," Shane corrected. "I hope you're not going to be burning through so many calories today that you'll need more than one of those a day. I found a case of them out back, tucked behind the wood. Looks like Mike Puller either shopped at the local Army surplus store, or he had a buddy who could get him the stuff for free. Either way, this stretches out our food supply."

"What's in it?" Scott asked. "Just the lasagna?"

Shane shook his head. "No. There'll be a powder mix for a beverage, some sort of snack, a bread product, and a desert. Also some matches, gum, wet-wipes, and a heater for the food. Lots of stuff we can use. If we have to."

"Did you eat yet?" Scott asked Courtney.

She nodded. "A little bit. Something called a Ranger bar. Basically a chocolate protein bar."

Scott was going to ask a little more, but his stomach growled. He took a sip of his coffee, winced at how hot it was, and blew on it to cool it down a little.

"I'm going to take a walk," Shane said. "I'll see you both in a bit."

When he had left by the back door, Scott turned to Courtney and asked, "What the hell were you doing in here with him?"

Courtney frowned at him. "Really, Scott?"

"Yeah, I mean, you got up and left me in there?"

"You were asleep," she said, her eyes going cold with anger. "What did you want me to do, sit there and hold your hand while you slept?"

Scott felt his face redden.

"And all I was *doing*, Scott," she said in a low voice, "was getting some coffee and a little to eat. What did you think I was going to be doing? Making out with him? You know, you act like you're in high school sometimes."

Scott forced himself to take a drink, in spite of how hot it was.

"I don't come down on you when you talk to a woman," Courtney continued, "so you sure as hell better not give me a hard time for talking to a man."

"Fine," Scott mumbled. "I'm sorry."

"Fine," Courtney snapped. She got to her feet.

"Where are you going?" Scott asked.

"Back to sit with Eileen and Dane. They're better company asleep than you are awake," Courtney said, and Scott groaned as she left the room.

Smooth, Scott, he chided himself. *Real smooth.*

Chapter 10: Wandering Where He Shouldn't

Dane had disengaged himself from Eileen's arm and slipped out of the house as he heard Courtney's voice raise up.

Dude will never learn, Dane thought, easing the front door closed. *Always harassing her. Told him before how Courtney won't put up with that.*

He looked around the front of the island, frowned at the sight of the yacht not a quarter mile off the pier, and turned his attention to the rest of Squirrel Island. Especially its lighthouse. The last time he had been in a lighthouse had been on the Marginal Way in Ogunquit, Maine. And he had still been in grammar school.

Dane walked over to the front of the lighthouse and saw the padlock on it was undone. The whole place was open for exploration. He grinned, slipped the padlock out of the latch, set it on the ground beside the door, and let himself in. The circular room he found himself in was dimly lit and wider than it seemed from the outside. A metal staircase wound its way up, protruding from the wall. From several windows scattered along the lighthouse's length, morning light drifted in.

Around the base of the building were boxes of supplies. Mostly electrical wiring, paint, all of the necessities needed to bring the buildings up to code and make them livable. There was even a stack of one-gallon water jugs, maybe thirty or forty altogether.

Dane walked over, grabbed one of the gallons and opened it. He drank long and deep from the tepid water.

Even though it's warm, Dane thought, *it still tastes damn good.*

He continued to drink for a minute, and when he had his fill, he capped it and returned it to the floor. He looked at the staircase, grinned, and started up it. The old metal groaned slightly beneath his weight, and a bit of panic flashed through him as he feared the whole assembly might pull out of the wall.

But it held.

With a sigh of relief, Dane continued up the stairs. Several times he hesitated, contemplated a retreat to the ground level again, but with each moment of hesitation, he shook off his fear.

When he reached the top of the lighthouse, he found himself beside the giant lantern. The old brass fittings were dull, and some were green with age. A radio with a handheld microphone was on a shelf, and the view from the top was nothing less than spectacular. Dane could see the coastline clearly, other boats and small ships sailing in the morning breeze. Down below, appearing deceptively close, lay the yacht. As he watched, the yacht swung out wide to the extent of her anchor, the line going taut.

"It's beautiful up here, is it not?"

Dane screamed with fear and surprise. He twisted around, his heart pounding.

A middle-aged man stood by the exit. He wore a thick knit sweater, corduroy pants, and heavy boots. He had a reddish brown beard, trimmed neatly, and a black cap usually seen in old pictures of early merchant captains.

However, the similarity ended there, for the man's eyelids were stitched open, the eyes black and the skin of his face cracked above the beard. His lips looked hard, as if formed from twisted plastic, the line of his mouth grim.

And Dane could see through him. The world behind the man was opaque, as though swaddled in fabric, but the man *felt* terribly real.

Dane cleared his throat and whispered, "Yes. It is beautiful."

"My name is Clark, and I am the keeper," he said. "I must ask, why are you here?"

"Um," Dane said, then he found his voice and said louder, "We went adrift last night. Put another anchor out and came in on the jolly boat. Trying to figure out what we're going to do now because someone stole the jolly boat last night."

"No one stole the jolly boat," Clark replied. "The others slipped your line last night and sent her out. She came back, of course."

"The boat's back?" Dane asked, surprised. "We can leave then!"

"Are you a shipwright?" Clark asked, a note of bitter humor in his voice.

"No," Dane said, slightly taken aback. "Why?"

"Alas, the scraps you'll find will not help you any," Clark chuckled. He turned his blank gaze out onto the water. "She came in hard, as they always do, and broke apart on the rocks."

Dane took a deep breath, prepared himself to ask another question and then thought, *Wait a minute. This is bull. I bet this is all a set-up. Some hidden camera. I bet it's just some sort of projector. There's no such thing as ghosts.*

"Sure they did," Dane said, relaxing slightly, glancing around and trying to spot the projector. *Just a joke. A bad one, but still a joke.*

An expression of surprise flickered across Clark's ruined face.

"Listen," Dane said, grinning, "you have yourself a good day. I'm heading back down to the keeper's house to see what other crap Shane has cooked up."

He stepped towards the stairs and Clark whispered, "Stop."

The word was spoken with authority, harshness, and a coldness which instantly brought Dane to a standstill.

"Where do you think you're going?" Clark asked.

"Out," Dane replied.

"No. We are bound here, for her to harness our strength. To build up her own." Clark said. The hands which had been kept clasped behind his back came out. They were thick, their backs and palms spider-webbed with fine, almost lace-like scars. And in the right hand was a knife of terrible, frightening design. It was curved like the moon in its last quarter. A deep gray handle, with a mirror image curved to the blade, was gripped tightly by Clark.

If, if this real, Dane thought, trying not to allow fear to dominate him, *then he's a ghost and he can't hurt me. Ghosts can't hurt me. They can't hurt anyone. Even the guy who offed himself, he did it himself. That's all. Be strong. No fear.*

No fear.

Dane straightened up and took a step closer to the stairs.

Clark advanced as well, saying, "I am the Keeper of the Lighthouse, and you will not leave until you have my permission to do so."

Dane let out a laugh, and then a moan of surprise and pain.

Clark's empty hand had swung out and smacked Dane solidly on the right cheek, the ghost's cold hand knocking Dane back and into the glass. He caught himself on the slight edge, horror growing in his heart.

"No, you shall go nowhere without my permission," Clark growled. "I am the Keeper, as surely as I was once captain. And let me tell you, my boy, there is nothing quite as fearful as a captain on his ship, or a Keeper in his lighthouse."

How can he hit me? Dane wondered, ignoring Clark. *How is it even possible? If he's a ghost. They can't hurt you.*

They can't hurt me.

But they did, Dane thought, reaching up and touching his sore, throbbing cheek. *He hit me hard.*

"I need to leave," Dane whispered. "I need to go back to my friends."

"No," Clark stated. "There's work here that needs doing. You look like a strong lad. Welcome to the Squirrel Island Lighthouse, boy."

"No," Dane whispered, then screamed, "No!"

He rushed for the stairs, but Clark met him there easily. The knife was a blur in Clark's hand, and he stepped deftly to one side. A sharp, terrible pain erupted in Dane's belly.

Dane fell sideways, landed first on his knees, then his hip, and finally his side. His head thunked loudly against the wooden floor, and he panted as he lay there. Fearfully, he reached down, touched his stomach, felt a warm, sticky liquid, and let out a sob.

When he brought his hand back up to examine it, he saw there was dark, rich blood upon it.

"Careful, lad," Clark said sympathetically. "It's a wicked blow I've dealt you. Reach much farther down and you'll feel your innards, which the Lord, in His magnificence, never meant for us to embrace."

Dane sobbed and felt something slip out of his stomach. He heard it slap wetly on the floor.

I'm going to die here, Dane realized morosely. *Oh God, I'm so sorry for everything I've done. I'm so, so sorry.*

"If you're praying, son," Clark said, putting his knife away and folding his arms over his chest as he stood there, "I'd say don't waste your breath. You will not leave this place. No, you're here forever, just like the rest of us. Since I've brought you over, though, well, you'll be with me."

Clark grinned. "Which is good. We have a great deal of work to be done in this lighthouse if we're to be getting it shipshape and Bristol fashion. Yes, a good deal of work."

Dane wanted to scream again, needed to scream again, but the pain was too intense. To even speak would have caused intense agony. Instead, all he could do was bleed out on the aged floor, and wait to die while his murderer kept a careful watch.

Chapter 11: And So It Begins

Shane stood on the pier and looked out at the yacht.

I need to get them off of this island, he thought. *This place is bad, and it's going to be too much for them. Might be too much for me.*

He reached back, patted the iron knuckles in his pocket, and sighed.

Yeah, Shane told himself, *it's going to get bad. I can feel it.*

A scream ripped out from behind him and Shane twisted around. Something stood at the top of the lighthouse. The shape was the barest hint of a person from where Shane was.

Why in the hell would one of them scream like that?

Courtney and Scott came out of the house, followed by the young woman, Eileen.

But not Dane.

Dane, Shane thought. He pulled the iron knuckles out, slipped them onto his right hand, and rushed up the slight incline to the lighthouse and found the door still locked. He kicked the door with all his strength, putting his foot close to the padlock. The force of his blow snapped the screws of the latch, and the wood ripped as the deadbolt tore through the aged and weathered wood.

The door sprang inward, bounced off of the inner wall, and shivered to pieces. Only a long, ragged edge was left, hanging madly from the old rusted hinges. Shane ran straight for the stairs and raced up, ignoring the way the metal quivered beneath his feet, or how the old bolts in the brick walls groaned.

Shane threw himself through the opening at the top of stairs and came to a sharp stop.

Dane lay on the floor, eyes wide in death while blood leaked out onto the floor. The young man's guts were in a slipshod pile, spilling out of the gaping hole in the boy's belly.

Shane's attention snapped from the dead youth to the ghost who stood off to one side, close to the mammoth lantern which served as the lighthouse's beacon.

The man smiled at Shane. "You're a fighter."

Shane nodded.

"They boy's dead."

"So he is," Shane said. "You killed him."

"It was required," the man said soberly. "Name's Clark. Clark Noyes. I'm the Keeper."

"Shane Ryan," Shane replied. "I'm here to find out why that was required."

"You'll need to speak to Dorothy," Clark answered. "If Dorothy will speak to you. You've been to sea, and not like this lad. No pleasure trip, aye?"

Below them, someone called his name and Shane yelled down, "Stay outside!"

"What ship?" Clark asked pleasantly.

"Depended on where I was and when," Shane replied warily, trying to keep his attention from Dane's pale, bloodless face. "Did a tour with the Sixth Fleet, though, Mediterranean."

"Sailor?"

Shane shook his head. "Marine."

Clark grinned. "Excellent. Well, if you'll excuse me, Shane, I've work to do, and so does this lad. As you can see, the lighthouse is in sorry shape. We'll have her righted soon enough, though. That we will."

The man vanished.

Work to do, Shane thought. He returned his gaze to Dane. The boy was dead. Undeniably so. But it seemed as though his spirit wouldn't be allowed to leave.

Dane had been enslaved.

Chapter 12: Horror

Scott stood outside the broken door of the lighthouse with both Courtney and Eileen. None of them spoke. They had all heard the scream. A terrible sound Scott was sure would haunt him for the rest of his life.

When they had raced outside, they had seen Shane down on the pier.

But no sign of Dane.

None.

Then Shane had run up to the lighthouse, kicked his way in, and gone after Dane. Scott and Eileen had hesitated at the entrance.

Courtney had not.

She had stepped into the old building and called up to Shane, who, in turn, had told them all to stay outside.

And so Courtney had gone back out, stood beside Eileen, and together the three of them waited, not so patiently, for answers. Scott could vaguely hear a conversation going on between Shane and someone else, but he couldn't make out any of the words.

It only lasted for a few minutes, and then Shane had called to them.

"I'm coming down now," Shane said from the top. "You need to stay back from the door. This isn't going to be pretty, and it sure as hell isn't going to be nice. Courtney?"

"Yes?" she said loudly, and Scott felt anger and jealousy rear their heads again as the older man said his girlfriend's name.

"Behind the house, by the wood, is a blue tarp. Grab it, will you?" Shane asked.

"Sure," Courtney said, and she hurried away.

"What's going on?" Eileen called out, desperation in her voice. "Is Dane up there with you?"

"Yes," Shane replied.

"Oh, thank God," Eileen said, her shoulders dropping in relief. Then she said, "Is he hurt?"

"He's dead," Shane answered.

"Oh Jesus Christ," Scott whispered. Eileen sank down to the ground, put her back against the old bricks of the lighthouse, and stared dully out at the Atlantic. And then Courtney was back, carrying the blue tarp with her. It was balled up in her arms. She glanced at Eileen and frowned.

"What's wrong?" she asked her friend.

Eileen shook her head.

"Dane's dead," Scott replied.

"What?" Courtney asked. "What do you mean he's dead? How can he be dead? We heard them talking up there."

Scott shook his head, unable to give her an answer.

"Courtney?" Shane called.

"Got it," she answered. "Now what?"

"Spread it out right in front of the door, please," he said. "And don't look, okay?"

"Okay," Courtney said. She brought the tarp to the door, stretched it out, and then turned to Eileen. "Come on, hon, let's go inside."

Her expression was one of dazed confusion, Eileen allowed Courtney to help her stand up. Together they went to the keeper's house.

Scott was alone.

"All set?" Shane asked.

"Yeah," Scott said. "And the girls went inside."

"Good," Shane said. "You may want to go inside too, Scott."

"No," Scott responded, his voice sounding oddly mechanical to his ears. "He's my best friend."

"Alright," Shane said. "Be ready."

A moment later, Scott heard Shane's footsteps on the stairs. They were heavier than before, and the man came down steadily. Soon, Scott could see him. Shane walked carefully, stepping on each riser. Once again, he was bare-chested, and blood stained his hairless flesh.

Dane Wesser, Scott's best friend, was limply draped over Shane's shoulder. Dane's body flopped and jiggled curiously, lifelessly with every step Shane took.

When the older man reached the ground floor, he grimly exited the lighthouse and gently placed Dane's body on the tarp. Scott could see why Shane was shirtless. The black tee shirt he had been wearing earlier was on Dane's stomach. Dane's braided tan belt had been removed from his khaki shorts, looped around the shirt and cinched tightly.

"Why?" Scott asked softly.

"Why what?" Shane asked, getting down on his knees.

"Your shirt?"

"To keep his intestines in," Shane said bitterly. "He was gutted like a fish."

Scott felt the urge to vomit, but he kept it under control. Silently, he watched Shane wrap the tarp around Dane, and then roll him carefully and gently in it. When he had finished, Shane looked up at Scott and said, "Will you help me move him?"

Scott nodded. "Where?"

"We'll bring him around the back. There's an old shed, it's seen better days, but it's empty. We can put him there until someone comes and gets us later, alright?"

"Yeah," Scott whispered. "Yeah, alright."

"Good."

Not really aware of what he was doing, Scott helped to pick up Dane, whose body was incredibly unwieldy, and together he and Shane went around the lighthouse. In the back was the shed, its door wide open and hanging cockeyed off of its hinges.

Shane backed in and said, "Here, on the right."

They maneuvered in the tight confines of the small structure and put Dane's body on a shelf that kept him off the ground and was barely long enough to fit him.

"Thanks," Shane said as they left the shed and he closed the door, sliding the latch in place. "Will you do me another favor?"

"Sure," Scott said numbly. "What is it?"

"Go in, grab a t-shirt out of my bag and bring it down to the pier?" Shane said. "I need to wash myself up. Salt water isn't great for it, but I won't waste what little fresh water we have."

"Yeah," Scott said. "I can do that."

"Thanks," Shane said. He hesitated, then he added, "Listen, I'm sorry this happened to your friend. I truly am, Scott."

Scott nodded, and Shane left for the pier.

Scott stood outside the shed a little longer. Then, with a shudder, he went into the keeper's house. He needed to get the shirt for Shane.

And he needed to tell Eileen about where Dane's body was.

His body, Scott thought, and tears filled his eyes. *Oh Christ, his body...*

Chapter 13: Down at the Pier

Shane was thankful the weather was warm, and that the breeze coming off of the ocean was equally warm. He had managed to scrub Dane's blood off of his body, and he sat on the pier, air-drying. The salt water had left an unpleasant residue on his flesh, but it was far more preferable than the remnants of Dane.

He took his cigarettes out, lit one, and exhaled as he looked at the water. The waves smacked the large stones at the base of the island. The water was rough, angry. A glance at the yacht showed it at the end of its tether.

It'll break free soon, Shane thought glumly, and he wondered when Marie might get out to them. He needed the kids, and the body, off of the island.

He heard footsteps on the path behind him and he turned quickly.

Courtney was approaching, holding his gray t-shirt in her hand.

"Fantastic," Shane said around his cigarette. "Thank you so much."

He got to his feet and walked towards her. She gave him a small smile as she handed it to him. He could see the fear and concern in her eyes.

After he had put the shirt on, he sat back down on the pier and she joined him. Several minutes of silence passed by before she asked, "What happened?"

"Dane was killed by a ghost," Shane said.

Courtney shook her head. "How? I mean, come on, how can a ghost hurt someone?"

"I don't know how," Shane said, then to himself, *No, she doesn't need to know.* "I just know they can. It's like bumble bees. They look like they shouldn't be able to fly, but they do. I don't know how a ghost can hurt someone, but they do."

Courtney hesitated, then she said, "How was he killed?"

"Badly," Shane answered. "We're going to leave it at that."

She nodded, accepting the reply. "Scott's not taking it well."

"They were good friends?" Shane asked.

"The best. They'd been friends since first grade," Courtney said.

Shane shook his head, finished his cigarette, and pinched out the butt. He stripped the paper off of the filter, tore up the filter, and then put the debris in his pockets.

"Most people would have thrown it in the water," Courtney said.

"Hm?" Shane asked.

"Your cigarette butt," she said. "They would have tossed it into the ocean."

"Old habits," Shane said, smiling. "They die hard."

The waves moved in, struck the rocks, broke apart, and then repeated the pattern.

"It's beautiful out here," Courtney said softly. "Too bad it's terrible, this place."

Shane nodded his agreement. "I have to find Dorothy."

Courtney frowned. "Who?"

"The ghost I spoke to last night before you all showed up," Shane clarified. "Clark, the one who killed Dane, he said she's in charge. I need to speak with her. But I need to find her first."

"Where do ghosts hide?" Courtney asked. "I mean, this is a small island. Where can they be?"

"Lots of places," Shane replied. "We've got the lighthouse and the keeper's house. The shed, and the pier. There has to be a cistern or something like it."

"For the water," Courtney said, nodding. "Yeah. There wouldn't be a well. They would have had to bring it in and store it here."

"And there's the cellar," Shane said, glancing back at the house. He saw Scott in the window, watching them.

"Scott's keeping an eye on you," Shane said.

"I know," Courtney said, sighing. She didn't bother to look. "He gets a little jealous. It's what I get for dating a guy four years younger than me."

"Strange that he gets jealous," Shane said.

"Why?" she asked.

"You don't strike me as the type of person who'd cheat," Shane said.

"I think you'd be more likely to tell him you were done and move on if you were interested in someone else."

"Yup," Courtney agreed. "That's me. He knows it too. I've told him. Doesn't mean he's listening to me, though."

Shane nodded.

"So," she said, "what do we do now, wait for your friends to notice you haven't written or replied?"

"Yes," he said. "Not much else to do about it. Just going to try and keep the rest of you safe. If I can."

"Thank you," Courtney said softly. "For all of us. I don't think either Eileen or Scott will see it that way, but I do. Thank you."

Shane nodded, trying not to look in her green eyes. After a pause, he said, "I need some coffee. How about you?"

"Sure," she said.

They both got to their feet and began the short walk back to the keeper's house. Scott was no longer at the window.

"Will you start looking for Dorothy right after coffee?" Courtney asked.

"Yup," Shane answered.

"What do you need?"

"Iron knuckledusters, light, and a whole lot of luck," Shane said.

"Where are you going to start?" she said.

"The cellar," Shane said.

They lapsed into silence, turning up the path towards the keeper's house. The sounds of their footsteps were swallowed up by the waves. Soon they reached the front door, and Courtney opened it for him. Shane smiled and nodded his thanks.

When he entered the house Shane saw Scott and Eileen sitting in the living room. Both of them were exhausted, deep shadows beneath their eyes, stubble on Scott's face.

"I'm going to make coffee," Shane said to them. "And I'll heat up some food. You'll both need to eat. Letting your bodies get too hungry or thirsty isn't the way to last this one out. Understood?"

Scott nodded.

"Eileen," Shane said sharply. The young woman looked up,

surprised. "Did you hear me?"

"No," she said softly. "I wasn't paying attention."

"You need to," Shane said grimly. "This place isn't nice. It isn't friendly. Whatever is here, hurts people. I need you to pay attention. I need you to eat. All of you. Not eating and not drinking is going to get you hurt, and probably me."

"Do you need help getting the food ready?" Courtney asked.

Shane nodded. "Any help would be great, Cort."

She blushed slightly at the nickname and passed by him to go into the kitchen. Scott's face reddened too, but it was from anger and not attraction.

Good, Shane thought. *Maybe it'll help him to pay more attention to her.*

Chapter 14: Angrier and Angrier

Scott didn't care about Shane having gone racing into the lighthouse after Dane. He didn't care the man was making them food.

All Scott cared about was the inappropriate amount of time Courtney, his girlfriend, was spending with a forty-something-year-old guy. Dane being dead didn't help Scott's attitude.

But it's all about 'Cort' now, he thought angrily. The pet name caused his anger to flare and his hands to itch. He had never wanted to hit anyone as badly as he wanted to hit Shane Ryan.

It would have been worse if Shane was actually hitting on Courtney in front of him. Shane wasn't though.

No, Scott fumed, *she's attracted to him. To a God-Damned forty-year-old!* he snarled inwardly. *Christ, she's in there helping him cook! She won't even let me near the stove at her place.*

Briefly, he contemplated sucker-punching Shane, but with the idea came the realization that if he didn't knock the man out, Shane would probably beat the hell out of him.

I just want to leave this place, Scott complained to himself. *Get good and far away, then we can figure out what the hell happened to Dane.*

The thought of his friend twisted his gut and Scott dropped his chin to his chest.

"Scott," Eileen whispered. "Did you hear that?"

He was about to say 'no' when he did hear something. A creak followed by a soft groan.

From the second floor.

Another creak filtered down, then a third.

Someone's walking up there, Scott realized.

Eileen turned toward the kitchen door, and he stopped her.

"Wait," he whispered.

She looked at him, surprised, and she asked in a low voice, "Why?"

"What if the person up there is a friend of Shane's?" Scott asked.

"I'm having a hard time believing all of this ghost stuff. Especially after Dane was killed."

Eileen hesitated, then she shook his hand off of her. "I don't believe it."

Scott watched her leave the room, and then he turned his attention to the stairs. The steps drew nearer. He got to his feet and walked softly over to the railing. The wood was cold and smooth beneath his hand. He held onto it as he peered up into the dim light of the second floor.

A man appeared, and Scott took a nervous step backward. It was the naked man he had seen on the pier the night before.

"Scott," Shane said, suddenly at his side.

Scott stared at Shane, unable to speak briefly. Then, finally, he managed to stutter out, "He's see-through."

"I know," Shane said. "Go on back, please. Let me speak with Mike here."

Scott could only nod as he backed up and found himself between Eileen and Courtney. In horrified, but fascinated silence, they watched the scene before them unfold.

Chapter 15: A Conversation

Shane slipped the iron knuckledusters onto his right hand, and he waited for the man at the top of the stairs to speak.

"You should leave," Mike Puller said.

"I'd like to," Shane replied. "Can't though. No reception for the phone. And someone decided to mess around with my ability to connect with the internet."

"She wants you gone," Mike said, moving a step closer.

"She can want me gone until Hell freezes over," Shane said pleasantly. "I'll leave as soon as I can."

"You'll leave now," Mike said, advancing another step.

"No," Shane said. "I won't kill myself like you did, Mike."

The statement caused the man to hesitate. "How do you know my name?"

"I'm a friend of Amy's cousin," Shane said. "I was asked here."

At the mention of Amy's name, Mike Puller lowered his head. "I'm sorry she has to carry this weight. I didn't want her to."

Puller fixed his eyes on Shane. "Doesn't mean you get to stay."

"I stay because I want to. And I'll leave when I want to. Do you understand me?" Shane asked. He drove all semblance of politeness from his voice. "I'm going to find out what the hell is going on, and then you're all going to leave. Am I understood?"

Puller chuckled. "You have no idea who you're dealing with."

"Cliché much?" Shane asked him.

Puller glared and raced down the stairs at him. Shane slipped to one side, and Mike Puller spun around and snapped, "Think you're clever? Think she won't find out about you?"

"Dorothy had best forget about me," Shane said softly, "and worry about learning to live with the living."

"The island is hers," Puller stated matter-of-factly. "The lighthouse is hers. The keeper's house is hers. You had best remember all of that."

"Go," Shane said. "You're boring the hell out of me. Go put some clothes on."

Mike Puller snarled with rage and hurled himself at Shane.

Shane didn't bother stepping aside. He adjusted his position, raised his right fist up and brought it smashing into Puller's face. The ghost's eyes went wide as the iron struck him.

A short scream pierced the air, and Mike Puller vanished.

Shane lowered his arm and wondered, tiredly, *When is Amy going to check her damned email and see I haven't written in?*

He sighed as he walked away from the stairs. Courtney, Eileen, and Scott all stared at him as he approached.

"What's wrong?" he asked them.

"You punched a ghost," Courtney said.

"Only worked because of the iron I had on. These knuckledusters," he said, slipping them off and putting them back into his pocket, "their iron, and a friend of mine gave them to me. Back when we had a little run-in with some other, equally unpleasant ghosts.

"Come on in the kitchen," he said as he passed by them. "I'll tell you what little I know about what can slow a ghost down."

They followed him, and as he and Courtney finished the preparation of the MREs, he told them about iron, and how to use it.

Chapter 16: Going Down

Scott was sulking in a corner, they had survived the night and the morning had slipped by uneventfully. Eileen lay on the sleeping bag, and Shane wasn't sure if the girl was awake or asleep. She was quiet, and she had cried again after they had eaten. Courtney had spoken with Scott, and whatever it was had resulted in his new bad mood. Courtney sat beside Eileen, her hand on her friend's shoulder. When Courtney saw Shane looking at her, she smiled.

Shane smiled back.

"When are you going to go into the cellar?" Courtney asked.

"In a little while," Shane replied.

"What do you think you'll find there?" she said.

"I'm hoping I'll find Dorothy," Shane said.

"Are you nervous?"

"Of course, I am," Shane said gently. "I'd be a fool not to be. I don't know what I'll run into down there. I know I've got a minimum of three ghosts to deal with, possibly more. It all depends on how many others Dorothy and Clark have bound to them. No, I'm not looking forward to this at all, Cort."

"Do you need me to go downstairs with you?" she asked. The fear was thick in her voice.

Shane smiled at her. "No. No, but thank you. I want you, Eileen, and Scott up here, where it's safe."

He stood up and stretched.

"Shane," Scott said bitterly, "what do we do if you get taken?"

"Set the house on fire," Shane replied. "And hope someone sees you and comes out to investigate."

He left them, passed through the kitchen, and went out the back door.

It was nearly mid-day, and the sun was strong and true. The island was warm, smelling sweetly of saltwater, and Shane wondered what he would find in the cellar of the house.

He walked around to the bulkhead, pulled it open, and set the locks. The stairs which led down were steep and narrow, the ledge of each barely more than ten inches deep. Webs clung to the corners, as did shreds of grass and the carcasses of long-dead insects. At the bottom was a tall, narrow door made up of long, thin boards bound together with old iron. Like the doors of both the lighthouse and the keeper's house, the door before him had once been blue as well.

Shane took a deep breath, calmed his heart rate, and armed himself.

Carefully, he descended the steps, reached the bottom, and thumbed the latch, swinging the door open.

Nearly pure darkness waited for him inside. The smell was rank and musty, a foul odor which threatened to burn the insides of his nose and caused his eyes to water. The daylight illuminated a small patch of earth which served as the cellar's floor. He stepped in cautiously, allowing his eyes to adjust to the limited light.

After several minutes of trying to adjust to the dark, he could make out rough shelves of canned and jarred food. In the ceiling above, he could see joists and the faint outline of a trap door. His skin crawled as he stepped in further. To the right, he saw four small boxes, one stacked on top of the other. At the bottom of the pile, though, was a fifth, larger box.

Shane stared at them. Blackness pulsed around them and sought to pull him closer. To drag him in.

"What are you?" he asked softly.

"We're death," a little girl answered.

"So our father called us," a boy added.

"Our mother too, Frederick," a different girl corrected.

"Yes, Jane," Frederick said.

Another child, an infant, let out a wail.

"You've awakened the baby," the little girl chided.

"Jillian," Jane said, "the baby never sleeps."

"It's why we're here," a man said.

"Yes, grandfather," Jane agreed. "It is why we're here."

"Why are you down here?" Shane asked.

"Punishment," their grandfather answered. "The children for being children. And myself for having the audacity to try and come between them and the discipline their parents sought to administer."

"They killed you," Shane said softly.

"Poison," the grandfather said sadly.

"Drowning," Frederick said cheerfully.

"Strangulation for the girls," Jane said.

"Who did it?" Shane asked.

"Father and mother," Jillian said, sounding as if she believed Shane to be a little too stupid.

Shane held back his exasperation and asked, "Could you tell me their names?"

"Mother and father," Jane said. "We knew them as nothing else."

"My son-in-law was Clark Noyes," the grandfather said. "My daughter was Dorothy."

"Where is she?" Shane asked. "I've come down here for her."

"Down here?" the grandfather asked, surprised. "Why would she be here?"

"She doesn't like the cellar," Jane said confidentially.

"She *hates* the dark," Frederick said. "Grandmother used to punish her by locking her in the cellar. For days on end, she would weep in the darkness. The door would be locked, and Mother would starve. Her disobedience kept her stomach empty, kept her in the cold depths. Grandmother sought to teach our Mother, although she would not learn.

"But, in the end, Mother took her anger out on Father. But only after Mother and Father had punished us," Frederick finished, laughing.

"How?" Shane asked.

"In the lighthouse," Frederick said, seeming happy to have Shane to speak with. "Oh, in the lighthouse, all the way up at the lantern. She brought him his coffee one dark night and knocked him unconscious. A terrible blow."

"Oh yes. She strapped him to the light, face first. She stitched his eyelids open, and over hours and hours she burned out his eyes. We could hear the screams from the top of the tower down here in our wooden tombs."

"It took days for him to die," their grandfather added. "I'm not even sure how many, only that he suffered tremendously. He would grow silent, and then my daughter would think of some new punishment for him. Some horrific bit of torment to inflict as much pain as she could on him."

Shane swallowed uncomfortably at the idea of torture. "Do you know where I could find her? Would it be in the lighthouse?"

"No, not the lighthouse," the grandfather replied. "Not if she can help it. She despised the lighthouse."

"Where then?" Shane asked.

"The second floor," Frederick answered.

Shane stiffened. "The second floor of the keeper's house?"

"Yes," she replied.

"It's only a large room up there," Shane said softly. "There's nothing."

"Perhaps not now," the grandfather said. "When we first moved into the keeper's house, there were two bedrooms in the loft."

"Mother's room looked out over the sea," Frederick said.

"She loved to see the shore," Jillian added.

Of course, it's the second floor, Shane thought numbly. *It's where she came down from. Just because the cellar felt bad didn't mean she was down here.*

The bodies are here.

Her own father and children, whom she murdered.

It's the death and the torture I felt. Their memories are sifting up through the stairs and into the back of the house.

And she's upstairs.

Upstairs!

"Thank you, for your time," Shane said as politely as he could. "I must go upstairs. I must see if Dorothy is in her room."

A scream from above cut him off and he was plunged into darkness as the cellar door slammed closed and locked itself.

Shane knew exactly where it was, and he threw himself at it, battering the wood as he sought to claw his way to freedom. A second scream rang out, and he managed to rip the old and rotten door off its hinges.

Biting back his anger, Shane went barreling up the stairs and into the sunlight.

Chapter 17: Dorothy Comes In

Courtney did her best to ignore Scott. He had tried to pull the whole 'I'm your boyfriend, you can't talk to him' speech earlier, but Courtney wasn't having any of it.

She sighed, shook her head, and focused her attention on Eileen. Her friend was still laying on Shane's sleeping bag, in and out of sleep, from what Courtney could tell.

Courtney removed her hand from Eileen's shoulder, brushed back a bit of hair from her friend's forehead, and felt an unnatural heat emanating from her flesh.

Oh no, does she have a fever? Courtney thought.

Muffled voices came from the cellar.

Children's voices.

Courtney looked over to see if Scott had heard them as well. His wide-eyed, surprised expression was enough of an answer.

Footsteps came down the stairs, and Courtney turned in time to see a woman finish her descent from the second floor. The woman's face was cold, merciless. There wasn't hate in her eyes, only disdain and disgust.

"This is my home," the woman said, facing them.

Courtney gasped, shivering as she found herself looking *through* the woman.

"We don't want to be here," Courtney said, her voice not nearly as confident as she would have liked. "We want to leave."

"But I don't want you to leave now," the woman said, smiling bitterly. "I like your company. In fact, I'm not sure I want any of you to leave. Ever. There's so much work to do to get the lighthouse ready. I need to be stronger. And for that, I need you. All of you."

She walked into the room, towards Courtney.

Courtney scrambled to her feet. Her heart beat ferociously in her chest and the impulse to run and fling herself into the Atlantic threatened to destroy her self-control.

"Get out of here," Courtney said, mustering all of the force she could. "Leave us alone."

"Soon enough," the woman said softly, "I will leave you all alone. But not yet."

Courtney was suddenly in the air, thrown back against the wall. Her breath was knocked from her, and she collapsed to her hands and knees. With her head spinning and gasping for air, Courtney heard Scott scream in terror. Beneath them, a door slammed shut.

Managing to take a deep breath, Courtney looked up and saw the stranger kneel down beside Eileen. Eileen, in turn, was sitting up, a groggy, confused expression on her face. Then she screamed as she saw the woman, who let out a pleasant, almost beautiful laugh.

Courtney tried to get to her feet, but only managed to collapse onto the floor. Her head spun too much from the force of the throw and she couldn't regain her balance. In horror, she watched as the stranger reached out, grasped Eileen by the head and smiled.

Eileen screamed again, tried to twist away, but the ghost kept a firm grip on her.

Something shattered outside, and the sound of running feet could be heard.

The woman slipped her thumbs onto Eileen's eyelids, and Courtney couldn't turn away as the stranger began to pry Eileen's eyes out of their sockets.

Eileen's screams turned to shrieks while Scott vomited and wept. Shane thrust open the back door. Courtney crawled forward, determined to stop the woman.

Then Shane raced out of the kitchen and past her.

"Dorothy!" he yelled.

The woman snarled at him. "You're all going to die," she hissed. "And sooner rather than later."

Even as Shane reached Dorothy, she grinned and twisted Eileen's head sharply to the left. The result was instantaneous and sickening. A dry, brittle snap.

Eileen's shriek ended abruptly, and she went limp.

Shane dove at Dorothy, his right hand smashing through her. With a howl of pure hatred, she vanished. Shane landed hard, rolled, and thudded against the wall, small pieces of plaster dropping onto him.

Courtney finished her crawl to Eileen. Her hand shook as she reached out, touched Eileen's neck, and sought a pulse.

There was none to be found. Dorothy had killed her.

Blood dried slowly on her friend's cheeks, her eyelids misshapen after the destruction of the orbs beneath.

Courtney began to shake uncontrollably. She pushed herself back and sat down. Shane moved closer, wrapped an arm around her, and pulled her in close. He said nothing.

She suddenly remembered Scott and looked over to him. He was passed out on the floor.

She relaxed into Shane's arms, smelled the sharp tang of blood on him. Courtney closed her eyes, felt sorrow and rage well up within her, and let out a long, angry sob.

Shane continued to hold her, and he let her cry. He didn't offer up soothing words, and he didn't pull away. He quietly stroked the back of her head, held her, and began to sing softly in a language she didn't know.

The steady thump of his heart accompanied the song, and Courtney wept for her murdered friend.

Chapter 18: Disbelief

Half an hour had passed since Eileen's death, and Scott's world continued to crumble

He stood in silence and looked out of the window at his father's yacht. He watched as it drifted away, the anchor line snapped and the sails furled. It rode the current, out towards deeper waters.

Maybe it'll be found, Scott thought numbly.

Everything was happening all at once. The yacht. Dane's murder. Eileen's murder.

And now this? he thought, turning to look at Courtney.

"How can you do this?" he asked her in disbelief.

Her face was stern, eyes red from crying, skin around them puffy. She had streaks of Eileen's blood on her, her arms folded across her chest.

"What do you mean?" she said coldly.

"How can you break up with me?" Scott asked, shaking his head. "I mean, how can you do it here? You couldn't wait until we got back to the mainland?"

"What?" she asked in surprise.

"Yeah," Scott said. "You don't think this is hard on me, too? Couldn't you think of me? You know, maybe that I shouldn't have to deal with the end of a relationship in the middle of all this crap?"

"What are you, fourteen?" Courtney snapped. "Jesus Christ, Scott, act your age."

"Why are you breaking up with me?" Scott demanded. "I thought everything was fine."

"Everything was fine," Courtney said. "Because we were dating. We're not engaged. We were dating. And now we're not."

"Is it because of Shane?" Scott asked in a low voice, not wanting the older man to hear him.

"Part of it, yes," she said. "Mostly, though, it's you acting like a teenager. And, you know, passing out instead of trying to help Eileen really doesn't qualify you as 'continued boyfriend' material."

His face burned with embarrassment. "It was a little too much to deal with."

"I managed to make an effort," Courtney said, biting off each word.

"This is garbage," Scott said angrily. "Our relationship isn't done until I say it's done. You'll see once we get back to the mainland. You're just stressed out."

He stopped as her expression changed.

Hatred filled her eyes.

"You listen to me, Scott," she whispered. "I've had one bad relationship where the guy wasn't going to let me go. He broke my wrist and my arm, then he cracked two of my ribs. He ate through a straw for months because I shattered his jaw with his laptop. He'll never, ever have children because of what I did to him. And let me tell you, *Scott*, you come near me, and I *will* hurt you. Do you understand me?"

Scott licked his lips nervously as he stepped back, bumping into the wall. He nodded. "I'm sorry."

"Shut up," she spat. "Just shut up." She turned around and went into the kitchen.

Scott stood alone in the living room. From outside, he heard the wind pick up, and the waves become louder. Slowly he sank into a sitting position. He dipped his head, closed his eyes, and asked himself, *How the hell did all of this happen?*

Chapter 19: A Good Idea Gone Bad

George Fallon steered his boat with one hand and kept his beer steady with the other. Vic Nato and Eric Powell sat in their seats, drinking their own beers. The fine, cooling spray of the Atlantic misted over them as George's new Boston Whaler, *Terminal Fleet*, cut through the water.

It was nearly six in the evening, and the sun had already begun its descent. But they were only five minutes from Squirrel Island.

"Pity about Mike," Eric said, raising his voice slightly to be heard over the thrum of the Whaler's powerful engine.

Vic, who didn't know Mike, stayed silent.

George, who had known Mike Puller since the first grade, spoke up. "Hated the guy."

"He was alright," Eric said defensively.

"Sure he was," George said, "if you were a broad. Otherwise, nah, he'd just as soon steal from you as work with you on a project."

"I heard," Vic chimed in, "he had screwed Nate Verranault on a job up in Bangor."

George nodded. "One of many. He found out what Nate bid on the carpentry, went in and told the owner he could do it in half the time, and for half the money."

"Didn't he go to prison for that one?" Vic asked.

"No," Eric said grumpily, "he went to Valley Street jail in Manchester. He didn't even do two years."

"Only because it was under five grand that he got away with," George said, chuckling. "Anyway, we'll be there in a minute or two. Got your phones all charged?"

Both Vic and Eric raised their beers in assent.

"Think this'll boost the website?" Eric asked.

George grinned. "Damned right, it will."

The three of them, with help from Vic's girlfriend, had started up a website. It specialized in photographs of death scenes. Accidents, murders, suicides. As long as death was involved, the pictures went up on the site. They had come onto the idea early one morning, talking about a construction accident Vic had seen.

All the wackos and weirdos who had come out of the woodwork, George thought. *Everyone trying to get a look, trying to take pictures.*

And the site is a damned goldmine, George grinned. With the money they made from subscriptions and advertisements, they were all enjoying life. George's new, 2017-model Boston Whaler was a prime example of it.

"There's the pier," Eric said, bringing George out of his pleasant reminiscing.

The new structure extended out into the ocean. George, who had been operating boats since his father stood him up behind the controls of an old speedboat when he was four, guided the Whaler in easily. Vic put his beer down, got to his feet, and was over the side in a moment, securing the boat to the pier as George turned the engine off. Eric, slightly unsteady on his feet, managed to get onto the pier and George followed.

"This the place?" Vic asked.

"Got to be," George said. "Only pier on the island."

"What the hell?" Eric said softly.

George turned towards Eric and saw the man was staring at the island. When he followed Eric's line of sight, he gasped in surprise.

At the end of the pier, sitting on a rock, was a boy of perhaps ten or twelve. He wore a pair of dark blue pants, battered shoes, and a collarless, button-down shirt. His skin was tanned, his hair bleached blonde by the sun. Sharp, bright blue eyes stared at George. The boy's face was thin and drawn. Between his narrow lips and clenched in his teeth was the stem of an unlit pipe.

The boy reached up, took hold of the briarwood bowl and took it out. He pointed at the three men, one at a time, with the pipe's stem.

I can see through him, George realized in surprise.

"Jesus Christ, George," Vic said softly. "Is the kid a ghost?"

"I think so," George whispered.

"This is awesome!" Eric said, barely able to keep his excitement contained.

George took his phone out, turned on the camera, brought it up, and snapped several pictures.

"Someone recording this?" Eric asked, fumbling with his own phone.

"I got it," Vic replied, holding his cellphone up.

The boy gave them a confused look, put the pipe back in his mouth, and said around it, "You're all going to die."

Eric chuckled, and Vic let out a laugh.

George felt his stomach tighten. He lowered his phone and asked, "What?"

"Die," the boy repeated. "Do you understand? We're going to kill you. All of you."

"Hey," George said to Eric and Vic, "maybe we should leave?"

"Are you kidding?" Eric asked.

"Come on, George," Vic said, grinning and glancing over at him. "Can you imagine the hits on the site when these go up? The video will probably go viral."

George looked back to the boy, who had gotten to his feet.

"No," George whispered, "this isn't going to go viral. This isn't going to go anywhere. He's going to kill us."

"Ghosts can't kill people," Eric said, grinning.

For the first time, George could hear the slur in Eric's words. The man had drunk more than George had known. A glance at Vic showed he was too giddy with the idea of being an internet sensation to recognize death was at the end of the pier. Death in the form of a little boy with an unlit pipe in his mouth.

The boy smiled. A quiet, disturbing smile which reminded George of his worst nightmares. The smile was a promise of pain, of misery, of pure terror right before the moment of death.

"We need to leave," George whispered. He left his friends on the pier and got back into the Whaler.

"Get in!" George shouted at Vic and Eric as he tried to start the boat's engine.

Vic and Eric looked at him, and the engine sputtered.

"Come on!" George said frantically, trying to start the boat again.

"George," Vic called, "relax, man, ghosts can't do anything."

George looked up at him and was about to argue the point when he saw the boy. The ghost was walking down the pier, humming softly to himself.

George recognized the tune. It was an old sea shanty, one his grandfather had used to sing. The boy was at the refrain.

I'll go no more a-roving with you, fair maid, George thought, hearing his long dead grandfather's voice.

"This is great," Eric said. "Absolutely fantastic!"

George tried again to start the engine, and again it refused to do more than sputter.

Vic continued to record, turning to follow the boy as he came to a stop in front of Eric. The boy looked up at Eric, who, in turn, bowed his head slightly to look into the boy's upturned face.

"You, on the boat there," the boy said, not turning away from Eric.

"Yes?" George asked, unsure of what else to do.

"You were smart," the boy said pleasantly. "You're the one who wanted to go. For that, you shall."

George hesitated, then he tried the engine again, and it started.

"Get in!" he shouted. He climbed up, untied the boat before he jumped back down.

"No," the boy said, his voice carrying with it a note of deadly seriousness. "They don't get to leave. Just you."

George went to protest, but he stopped.

The boy, with his right hand straight as a knife's blade, plunged it straight into Vic's stomach.

Vic stiffened, dropped the phone, and gasped in shock and pain. He convulsed slightly, tried to breathe but couldn't. The ghost grinned and turned his arm gently to the right.

Vic's scream echoed off of the stones, and the door to the keeper's house was flung open.

Enough! George screamed to himself. He turned the wheel hard to starboard, slammed the throttle down, and the Whaler fairly leaped away from the pier and back to the open sea.

More of them in the house, he thought frantically, aiming for the mainland. *Oh, Jesus, there's more than one.*

Fear drove him away, and he abandoned his friends to their fates.

Chapter 20: Things Get Worse

Shane had heard far too many screams. The newest one was completely unexpected.

He had finished moving the unfortunate Eileen into the shed to lay alongside Dane, who had already begun to decompose in the June heat.

He had rinsed the taste of death out of his mouth, spat it out on the ground, and thought he had heard the sound of an engine.

Shane straightened up and thought, *Did they send someone a day early?*

He grinned, thrilled with the idea, and he hurried to the front of the keeper's house. He quickly ran around the corner as Courtney was coming out the front door. Down on the pier, Shane saw three people. Two of them were men, and one of them a child. The men were alive, and the child was not. A large, deep-sea fishing boat turned away from the pier and raced out into the sea.

Shane's excitement at a possible rescue vanished.

"Stay up here, Cort," Shane said, motioning for the young woman to stay back.

She gave him a nod and Shane ran down the slight rise to the pier. He held his horror in check as the child, a boy with a pipe, pulled his hand out of one man's stomach. As the stranger collapsed to the pier, the boy advanced on the second man, who backed up, holding his hands out in front of him.

"Stop!" Shane yelled, his boots hitting the wood of the pier.

The boy turned, grinning around the stem of the pipe. Behind him, the man turned and ran, diving into the ocean.

Shane watched as the boy's shoulders slumped and he turned fully to face him. The boy took his pipe out of his mouth, pointed at Shane, and said, "You've ruined my fun, you have!"

"Have I?" Shane asked, catching a glimpse of the man swimming away. "Let me call him back."

"The other? I think not. He's too afraid, he is."

The swimmer dipped beneath a wave and didn't appear again.

"And," the boy grinned, "he didn't swim out far enough. Not nearly. There are a few of us in the rocks beneath the waves. He's joined them now."

Shane forced his thoughts away from the drowned man, glanced at the man lying on the pier and saw he wasn't dead. Severely injured, but not dead.

"What's your name?" Shane asked.

"Ewan," the ghost said, and he spoke a sentence in a different language.

Gaelic, Shane realized, translating it quickly.

Shane replied in the same. "I would have to argue, Ewan. I *do* know who my father is."

Ewan's eyes widened, and then the boy grinned. Still, in Gaelic he said, "So you speak the mother tongue, do you?"

Shane nodded.

"It is a pleasure to hear it," Ewan said, smiling pleasantly. "Never did I expect to hear it again. I have been here a long time, Shane Ryan."

"You know my name?" Shane asked, keeping an eye on Ewan as he took a small, careful step towards the downed man.

"We know your name here," Ewan said. "We were told to expect you."

Shane stopped and looked at the boy. "Told by whom?"

"By Dorothy, of course," Ewan said. "She knew you were coming. I wouldn't worry about the man behind me, Shane. He's not long for this world, although he shall be in mine soon enough, don't you know it?"

"What did you do?" Shane asked softly, hoping the boy was lying.

"I pushed and pulled, prodded and poked," Ewan said in a sing-song voice. "I rearranged a few things. To be honest with you, Shane, I'm surprised he's still breathing air."

"Is there no way to save him?" Shane said.

Ewan shook his head. "And it is not his fate to be saved. Fear not, each of us has our destiny. His is to be here, with us."

"And what is mine?" Shane asked.

"None of us have heard about your fate, Shane. Not even Dorothy.

But she would like to pretend she has," Ewan said with a wink. "Now, if you will excuse me, I have a bit of a schedule to keep."

Before Shane could react, Ewan turned around, took hold of the man on the pier, and dragged him into the ocean.

Shocked, Shane could do nothing more than watch as the man vanished into the depths.

What the hell is going on here? Shane wondered. He remained there for another minute until he heard Courtney calling his name.

Shaking his shock off, Shane turned and made his way back up to the keeper's house.

Chapter 21: A Phone Call is Made

"So," Uncle Gerry said, sitting down and smiling at her. "What's new with you?"

Marie Lafontaine shrugged, relaxed, and said, "Not much."

"Have you seen Shane lately?" her uncle asked, a falsely innocent note in his voice.

"I did, as a matter of fact," she replied, frowning. "Why do you ask?"

"No reason," he said, dropping a hand to his dog's head and scratching the German Shepherd between the ears. "None at all."

"You wouldn't be pushing to have us start dating again, would you?" she asked.

"Would I ever do such a thing?"

"You would," she answered, "and you have."

"I thought you two would get along well together," Uncle Gerry said.

"We do, and we did," Marie said. "We're not compatible."

"You make it sound like a chemistry problem," he said.

"If you want to boil it down, Uncle Gerry," she said, sighing, "that's exactly what it is. We like each other. We have a good time when we go out. I don't want to date him. He doesn't want to date me. Even if we did, and if we got married, there is no way in hell I would live in his house. Pretty certain he won't leave it either."

Uncle Gerry harrumphed, took a drink of coffee, and shook his head. "Too bad. I'd like to see you married, someday."

"How about I just shack up with someone for a while?" she asked teasingly.

He rolled his eyes. "Don't get me started, Marie."

She chuckled and said, "Back to the first question, yes, I saw him earlier this week. You know Amy bought the lighthouse, right?"

"Your cousin on your father's side?" Uncle Gerry asked.

Marie nodded. "Yeah. She had a little bit of trouble with her contractor and Shane said he'd help her out."

"Has he said how it's going?" her uncle asked.

"No," Marie said. "I have to call Amy in a little bit. They're supposed to keep in touch with one another. No cell phone reception on the island, so they're using e-mails."

Turk, her uncle's dog, stood up and looked patiently at Gerald.

"Really?" Uncle Gerry said. "I just poured my coffee."

"Why do you talk to your dog?" Marie asked. "You know you sound crazy, don't you?"

"What do you want me to do?" he replied, putting his mug down on the coffee table. "He asked to go out, you want me to ignore him?"

Marie shook her head as her uncle stood up, wincing slightly.

"Come on, Turk," Uncle Gerry said, motioning to the dog. "Let's go."

Turk walked slowly behind her uncle, and soon she heard the back door open. She took her cell out, pulled up Amy's number, and dialed it.

After two rings, her cousin answered.

"Hey, Marie!" Amy said cheerfully.

"Hey Amy," Marie said, grinning. "Any word from Shane?"

"Hold on," Amy replied. "I'm just getting to this morning's emails. Had a late start to the day."

Marie listened to the clack of fingers on a keyboard, then Amy said, "Okay, here we go. Hm, looks like there's nothing going on. He says he's checked the house, and the shed. No ghosts yet. Shane also said he'll be checking the lighthouse itself. He'll shoot me an email as soon as he finishes up with it.

"And," Amy said happily, "I'll send you a text as soon as the email comes in. You worried about him?"

"Of course," Marie replied, surprised.

"You two a couple or something?" Amy asked slyly.

Marie found herself blushing. "No, Amy. Christ, you and my uncle Gerry are absolutely terrible about Shane."

"Even without his hair, he's a pretty good-looking guy," Amy said, snickering.

"Lay off," Marie said. "Anyway, you'll shoot me a text?"

"Guaranteed," Amy replied.

"Great," Marie said. "Thanks, Amy."

"No," Amy said, "thanks for sharing him. I really appreciate what you're both doing to help me out."

"You're welcome. I'll talk to you soon," Marie said. She ended the call and put the phone away. From the back of the house, the rear door opened and the click of the dog's claws on linoleum could be heard.

Uncle Gerry and Turk came into the room, resumed sitting at their previous seats, and her uncle said, "Were you talking to someone, or was I hearing things?"

She grinned. "No, you weren't hearing things. I gave Amy a quick call. Shane's fine."

"Good," Uncle Gerry said. He leaned back into his chair, saying, "Tell me, what's new and exciting in this fair city of ours?"

"Nothing," she said. With a sigh, she began to tell him about the rise in gang violence and drug-related crimes.

Chapter 22: Feeling Isolated

Scott had never felt so alone before. Not even when he had been forced to sleep in the musty old sub-basement of the Upsilon-Upsilon House when he was a pledge.

Courtney was asleep on the kitchen floor. Scott sat on the countertop, and Shane stood in the doorway of the living room. The older man lit a cigarette, inhaled deeply, and then let out a long, steady stream of smoke.

Didn't even ask to see if I minded, Scott thought angrily.

Shane looked at him, and Scott turned his head quickly.

"Come on," Shane said. "Let's go out front."

The tone of the man's voice told Scott it wasn't a request, but an order. A command from a man who seemed to have been used to commanding.

Angrily, Scott got up and followed Shane outside. Once in the cool, night air, Shane gestured for Scott to sit down. Scott sat on the front step and glared at Shane.

Shane's face was a perfect mask of calm. His eyes shined in the starlight. The anger in the man's gaze forced Scott to swallow nervously, his own emotion subsiding. He lowered his eyes, cleared his throat, and asked, "Why'd you want me out here?"

"Because we need to talk," Shane answered.

"About what? 'Cort?'" Scott said, spitting out the last word.

"It would be best if you calmed down," Shane said softly. The deadly seriousness in the man's voice made Scott swallow uncomfortably. "Do you understand me?"

Scott nodded.

"Good. This is not about Courtney. Whatever is going on between you two, is just that; something going on between the two of you," Shane paused a moment as if allowing Scott to comprehend what he had said. "This is about the three of us, this island, and the ghosts who are here. I want to move us out of the house and into the lighthouse

74

soon. I don't trust the house anymore, not with Dorothy living upstairs. I'm not certain as to who's in the lighthouse, but we'll move in and find out."

"Dane was killed in the lighthouse," Scott said in a low voice.

"Yes," Shane agreed. "And Eileen was killed in the house. Got five other ghosts in the basement, one on the second floor, and possibly one in the lighthouse. Let's not forget there are at least three dead from the pier. There are ghosts and bodies all over this damned island. I would feel better about going into the lighthouse. If you want to stay in the keeper's house, then I'll give you some supplies, and you can wait it out there."

"I will. I'm not leaving the house for anything. I don't want to be in the lighthouse. It's where my best friend died. What about Courtney?" Scott asked, finally looking up at Shane again.

Shane shrugged. "I think she's a smart woman. She'll make up her mind and go where she thinks is best."

A spark of hope ignited within Scott. He straightened up. "When are you moving into the lighthouse?"

"In a bit," Shane said. "I'm going to try and get a hold of the owner again, see if the internet connection is back up."

"I don't even know why it would be out," Scott said angrily. "Even without any phone service we should be able to go online."

"Regardless," Shane said, finishing his cigarette and rubbing the butt out on the ground. "I'm moving in. First, I'll divvy up the supplies."

Without another word, Shane slipped past Scott and returned to the house. Scott sat on the front step, looked out at the haze in the sky, and smiled.

She'll stay with me in the house, Scott told himself, nodding. *I know she will.*

Chapter 23: Getting Worried

Shane still couldn't access the internet. The laptop wouldn't power up. And neither would his phone. He stood in the kitchen, both of the devices on the counter, and he tapped his fingers lightly. The urge to light up another cigarette was strong, but he resisted.

God forbid I run out of the damned things, he thought.

Courtney snored suddenly and opened her eyes tiredly. She blinked several times, then rolled over and went back to sleep.

Shane smiled at her.

Her presence alone made him happy, which was strange.

And she's way too young, Shane thought, shaking his head. It felt odd to be attracted to someone her age. He let the thought slide away and focused on the task before him. He needed to get his supplies into the lighthouse. Above him, he heard noises, and he wondered if Dorothy or the naked Mike Puller might wander down the stairs again.

Why will the lighthouse be safer? he asked himself.

Because Dorothy's not here, and she's the worst one around.

He looked at the stack of MREs on the counter. Adding them to the food he had brought, between the three of them, they had enough to last four days.

If we stretch it, he added silently.

Bottled water had been found in the basement of the lighthouse. All they needed to do was either wait for Amy, or whoever she sent, to rescue them from the island.

"Shane?" Courtney asked tiredly.

He turned and smiled at her. There were sleep lines on her right cheek, from where she had rested her head against his rolled up sweatshirt.

"Hey," he said. "How are you feeling?"

"Like I've been thrown down a flight of stairs," she answered, yawning. Then, in a darker tone, she asked, "Where's Scott?"

"Living room," Shane answered. He took a bottle of water out of his bag and handed it to her. She nodded her thanks, opened it, and took a long drink.

When she had finished, she asked, "What's going on?"

"I'm getting ready to move my stuff into the lighthouse," he replied.

"Why?"

He explained his reasons quickly and at the end she nodded. "I'll go with you."

"You don't feel safe here?" Shane asked.

She shook her head. "Not to sound corny or anything, but I feel safer with you."

He felt his face go red, and she smiled at him.

Scott walked into the kitchen. He looked coldly at Shane, then he turned his big, love-struck eyes to Courtney.

The affection was not returned.

Whatever feelings she had for him before this are gone, Shane realized.

"Shane's moving into the lighthouse," Scott said. "You and I are staying here."

"I think you're a little confused," Courtney said. "You're staying here, and Shane and I are going to the lighthouse."

"I figure we can set up a—" Scott paused, furrowed his brow and said, "I'm sorry, what did you say?"

Courtney repeated herself.

Scott's face went nearly purple with anger. His eyes, rage-filled, moved rapidly from Courtney to Shane and back to the woman.

"You can't go with him," Scott sputtered, nearly choking on his words.

"I can," Courtney replied, getting to her feet. "And I will. If Shane says it's not safe here, then it isn't safe here, Scott. Not only does he know a lot more about this stuff than we do, but he's also the only one who's been able to do something about it."

"So that makes him more of a man than me?" Scott snarled.

Shane kept a careful eye on the young man.

"No," Courtney answered. "It means we should stick with him because he knows what he's doing."

"I'm not going in there with some twisted, bald psycho," Scott spat, "and definitely not with any whore!"

Shane stepped forward. Scott raised a fist, swung clumsily at him, and Shane blocked it easily. A casual movement of his left arm and Scott's punch bounced haphazardly away.

Shane's punch was not clumsy, and Scott didn't block it.

The blow was delivered precisely, and with the barest amount of power to let Scott know he had been hit. The younger man's head snapped back, his teeth clicking together loudly. Scott stumbled into the living room, but Shane didn't follow.

He stood in the doorway, his hands held loosely at his side.

"Are you done?" he asked as Scott straightened up. A small trickle of blood leaked out of Scott's right nostril.

"You hit me," Scott said with surprise.

"You tried to hit him!" Courtney yelled.

"Shut up!" Scott said, stepping forward and pointing at her.

Shane reached up and took hold of Scott's index finger.

"Stop it," he said softly to the young man.

"You and your whore—"

Scott didn't finish.

Shane bent the finger back sharply, causing the young man to screech and collapse to his knees, arm above his head. Shane was close to breaking the digit, but he held back.

"Scott," Shane said, relaxing the tension.

Scott looked up, tears of rage and pain mingling freely in his eyes.

"Are you listening to me, Scott?" Shane said.

Grimacing, Scott nodded.

"Good," Shane said. "Now I want you to understand something, in case you haven't figured it out on your own. I do not appreciate you calling Courtney names. Is that understood?"

"Yes," Scott replied through clenched teeth.

"Excellent," Shane said. "Here's a little information for you. I served in the Marines for twenty years. I did some exceptionally bad things. And I liked them. I liked them a lot. I can hurt you in ways which will never show, and I can cause you pain you can't even imagine."

Shane bent the finger back a hair's breadth and Scott whimpered.

"Do you believe me, Scott?"

"Yes," the young man whispered.

"I'm glad." Shane let go of Scott and the young man instantly cradled his injured finger. "I'm going to leave you enough food and water for several days. If I hear anything about someone coming to take us off of this island, then I will tell you. If you're in trouble, come on over to the lighthouse, or yell for me. If you get afraid, come on over to the lighthouse. I won't hold a grudge."

Scott got to his feet, glared at both Shane and Courtney, then he turned and left the house by way of the front door.

Shane went back into the kitchen, where Courtney was already dividing the food.

"I'm sorry," Shane said.

"Don't be," Courtney said, giving him a grim smile. "He's a jerk."

"Fair enough," Shane said.

In silence, they prepared to go over to the lighthouse.

Chapter 24: In the Waterman

George Fallon sat alone at the bar of the Waterman. He had finished three bottles of Budweiser, and three double shots of whiskey. Behind him, the lights of the wharf glowed brightly against the night sky. A few regulars were in the bar, but there was a new bartender, some young guy that George had never seen before.

George didn't look at him too much.

He'll cut me off soon, George thought dully. *And then what'll I do?*

He couldn't drive the image of the kid on the pier out of his head.

George couldn't forget about how he had abandoned his friends.

Are they even alive? he wondered. *What did I do?*

The bell over the entrance rang, and George glanced into the mirror behind the bar. Around the bottles of top-shelf liquor, he saw an attractive blonde woman walk in.

George couldn't be bothered with her, though. He needed another drink.

He looked up to the bartender, but the caution in the kid's eyes told George he'd be lucky to get a seltzer water.

"You look like a drinking man," the blonde said as she sat down next to George.

He nodded and straightened up a little. She smelled of sweetness and roses.

"What are you drinking?" she asked him.

"Whiskey with a beer chaser," George answered.

She smiled and let out a light, beautiful laugh. "I like the sound of that."

She raised a perfectly toned and tanned arm, gesturing for the bartender. The young guy hurried over.

"Hello," the bartender said, smiling. "What are you drinking tonight?"

"Give me a pair of whiskeys and two beers. Whatever you have on tap," she answered, putting a small purse on the bar.

The young guy frowned and said, as politely as he could, "Miss, I was about to shut him off. He's too drunk to drive anywhere."

"Don't worry about that," she said, almost purring. With a delicate hand, she opened her purse, took out several twenties and handed them over. "I'll be taking him home tonight. And I don't need the change."

The bartender, George saw, was no fool. He nodded, got the drinks, gave George and the woman a pleasant smile, and went down to the other end of the bar.

She raised her whiskey and George did the same.

"To new friends," she said, and they clinked their glasses together.

He knocked the drink back and was impressed to see she did the same.

"So," George said, taking a drink of beer, "what's your name?"

"Let's have a little mystery, right now," she said with a wink. "My only question for you is, do you have a boat, and is it big?"

George let out a laugh, finished half of his beer and said proudly, "Sweetheart, ain't nothing small about George Fallon."

"I was hoping you'd say something along those lines," she said, grinning. "Drink up, George, then maybe you can take me out on your big boat."

George finished his beer, and she signaled to the bartender for another round.

Things are looking up, George thought drunkenly.

The bartender set another whiskey in front of him, and George smiled as he picked it up. All thoughts of Vic, Eric, and even the little ghost were gone from his mind as he looked at the woman beside him.

Yes, George thought, knocking it back. *Things are looking up.*

Chapter 25: In the Lighthouse

Shane didn't like the lighthouse. Granted, he disliked the keeper's house more, but the lighthouse was a close second.

Courtney felt the same way.

"You okay?" he asked her.

She nodded, her gaze traveling up the stairs. "Do we need to go up there?"

"Maybe tomorrow night," Shane answered. He sat down beside her, draped his arms over his raised knees, and looked up to where the young man, Dane, had been killed.

"Why tomorrow?" Courtney asked. "Why not today?"

"I'm hoping someone will come and check on me in the morning," Shane said. "I haven't checked in since I arrived."

"And if they don't come?" Courtney said.

"Then I break the lantern," Shane said. He fished out his cigarettes, lit one, and blew the smoke away from her.

"Why not now?" Courtney asked.

"It's too risky," Shane said.

She was silent for a short time before she said, "Because if you shatter the light and there's already a rescue crew on its way, they might not be able to get to us."

He nodded. "Exactly. If we break it tomorrow during the day though, whoever monitors the light on the mainland will send a boat out immediately. It has to be standard procedure because the lights are always on, they have to be for safety. Which means there has to be a boat on standby at all times. More than likely, a Coast Guard patrol boat. Maybe even a cutter. But there'll be one ready."

"And they'll take us off the island," she said softly.

"I hope so," Shane said.

"What about the bodies?" Courtney said, looking at him. "Eileen's neck was broken. Dane was ripped apart."

"I'll deal with the fallout of their deaths," Shane said, the cigarette trembling in his hand briefly. "I don't want to go to prison for a couple of murders I didn't commit, but I'd rather be alive than dead and trapped here forever."

"You think that's what happens?" she asked softly.

"I do," Shane said. "When I was up there, the ghost who killed Dane said he needed help to clean the lighthouse. I'm assuming that was why he killed Dane."

"What? Like some undead indentured servant?" she asked, her voice quivering with a hint of revulsion and fear.

"Exactly."

"What if he needs more?" she asked, trembling. "What if one isn't enough?"

Shane reached out a hand, and Courtney took it.

"We're in here together," he said softly. "We'll be okay. We know what to look out for."

She hesitated and then asked, "What about Scott?"

"Scott has a choice to make," Shane said gently, without any malice. "He can come and be safe with us, or he can sulk in the keeper's house. It's really his decision."

"Yeah," she whispered. "You're right."

Courtney leaned against him, pulling his arm up and around her shoulders.

"What do we do now?" she asked.

"Now," he answered, "we wait to see what happens, if anything."

"Do you think it'll be a quiet night?" she asked hopefully.

"No," he said with a shake of his head. "I think someone will come in, and they'll be coming for us. Maybe more than one of them. But we'll be okay.

"How do you know?"

He kissed her forehead lightly. "I know."

She nodded her acceptance of his statement, closed her eyes, and rested her head against his chest. Shane enjoyed it. He felt strong, but he knew the dead were coming and he needed to be prepared.

Of that I have no doubt, he thought, sighing.

Shane tugged the knuckledusters out of his back pocket, slipped them on, and flexed his fingers.

The girl fell into a light and fitful sleep, waking occasionally to look around and adjust her position.

Shane remained awake.

He chain smoked, careful not to drop ashes on Courtney. The base of the lighthouse was cool, the bricks and stones stained with age. Gallons of water were stacked along one portion of the wall, various tools and equipment a little further along.

Who'll pay us a visit tonight? he wondered. *And how many?*

What's Scott doing? Shane thought. *Will he survive the night?*

Chapter 26: In the Keeper's House

Scott had literally backed himself into a corner. He sat on the floor in the kitchen, knees pressed against his chest. He was able to see into the living room and out the back door from where he was.

Shane and Courtney had taken the only light with them. Every few seconds, the house lit up with the glow of the rotating lantern in the lighthouse.

Scott shivered, not from the weather, but from the steady creak of the floorboards above him. He wasn't alone in the house.

Stop, he thought, staring at the ceiling. *Oh God, won't you please stop walking?*

He pictured the woman, Dorothy, and how easily she had killed Eileen.

She's going to come down here and kill me, Scott thought, panic building up within him. *I know she is. She's going to do the same to me. She's going to pop my eyes and snap my neck. Or worse. Oh, Jesus! It's going to be worse.*

Go to the lighthouse, he thought. *Go. Just go. No shame. Shane told me I could. Even Courtney wasn't being a jerk. Just go. Go. Go!*

Scott hyperventilated as he sat in the kitchen, staring at the ceiling. He let his legs go slack, and he tried to stand up. As soon as he did, the noises above him changed.

The footsteps paused, then they moved away.

Towards the stairs, Scott realized, scrambling to his feet. *She's coming down.*

Trying to get a handle on his fear, Scott turned to the back door. He had left it open to make certain he could run if he needed to.

Yet as he looked at the exit, a small boy blocked the doorway. The child was thin, see-through, a wicked apparition. As the dead youth stepped into the kitchen, the door slammed closed behind him.

"No," the boy said gently, "you'll not be leaving this way. Not tonight, no."

The stairs groaned with an unseen weight.

I can make it to the front door, Scott told himself, each breath shallow and nearly futile. He took two small steps towards the living room, and when the boy didn't follow, Scott's courage was bolstered. He turned his back to the ghostly intruder and hurried into the living room.

As he entered it, the naked ghost of the man who committed suicide grinned at him.

"It's not so bad here, Scott," the man said, taking a step forward. "You'll like it here. I know I do. Oh, the promises she's made. You'll do your time like I'm doing mine, but when it's done. When it's done, Scott, yes, *then* we'll have our glory."

Scott stifled a scream and raced for the front door, he shoved it wide open, stumbled over the threshold and fell face first into the grass. He got back up and let out a shriek.

Dane stood before him.

His friend wore the clothes he had died in. The shirt was slashed open diagonally, and his belly was sliced open the same way. Scott could see into his friend's stomach. He could see the intestines, gray and bloated like a hideous, coiled worm.

Dane winked at him and asked, "Why are you running, Scotty?"

Scott tried to answer, to form words, yet his lips only trembled.

"You know what they say about running, don't you, Scotty?" Dane asked pleasantly.

Scott could only shake his head in reply.

"They say not to," Dane said. "And do you know why?"

"No," Scott whispered.

"Ask why?" Dane said, grinning.

"Why?"

"Because you'll die tired," Dane said. He laughed, shook with pleasure at himself. Scott turned and threw up as his friend's intestines spilled out onto the ground. Hot bile splashed onto Scott's hands and forearms. The thick beef stew he had eaten cold from the MRE was hot and stinking in front of him. When he looked up, he saw Dane's ghostly innards on the ground.

Scott scrambled backward, got to his feet and looked around desperately. The naked man was in the doorway to the keeper's house. Behind Dane was the lighthouse.

The lighthouse, Scott thought frantically.

I need to get to the lighthouse.

Dane wasn't going to let him by. Scott could see it in his dead friend's eyes.

Scott looked over his shoulder and gasped.

Eileen was only a few feet away. Blood trickled down from beneath her misshapen eyelids. Her neck was wrong, something off about the way she held her head. Her dead lips spread into a wide smile before she said, "How do I look, Scott? Still pretty enough for your best friend?"

Scott tried to run, but his feet became tangled up together. He fell, hit the ground hard, and rolled down the small hill towards the pier. As he rolled, he caught sight of others on the pier. Twenty of them, maybe more.

He flung his arms out, managed to stop himself and got up, his stomach aching and his head pounding. His eyes locked onto the door of the lighthouse, and he launched himself towards it.

A terrible cold slammed into him, knocked him to his knees and swarmed, over him. Hands pulled at his limbs, his clothes. Yanked his hair out of his head and smothered his screams as the breath was stolen from his lungs. Hardened fists slammed into his flesh, sought out the soft parts of his body and punished him, relentlessly, without mercy.

Scott could hardly think, and part of his mind screamed for the solace of unconsciousness.

No such peace was granted.

When he felt as though he could bear no more, it ended.

The cool grass caressed his face, and dimly Scott realized he was naked. Completely stripped of his clothing.

He shivered uncontrollably, a piercing cold pulling at his nerves, threatening to pull each delicate, sensitive tendril from him.

"Look at me."

Scott lifted his head and saw Dorothy. She stood before him, her face hard and impassive. There was no hint of sympathy. No whisper of mercy.

Through her, he could see the lighthouse, the tall structure was a place of sanctuary.

And I said no, he thought, tears welling up in his eyes.

Dorothy bent down and reached for him.

Scott closed his eyes and managed a hoarse scream as she pried open his mouth, and tore the lips off.

Chapter 27: Listening to Things Best Left Unheard

Courtney slept through most of it, thankfully.

She lay on the stone floor of the lighthouse, her head on Shane's lap as he drank his whiskey straight from the bottle. He moved it out of the way as she sat up swiftly, her eyes wide and full of horror.

"What was that?" she asked, all vestiges of sleep gone from her.

"Scott," Shane said. He capped the whiskey and put the bottle down.

"What are they doing to him?"

"Torturing him," Shane said bitterly.

She looked at him, her face pale. "We need to do something."

"All I could do now," Shane said, "is kill him, if I could even get close enough. There are too many of them."

"What?" she said. "I thought there were only a few."

Shane shook his head. "I looked out when I heard his first scream. There's at least thirty, maybe more by now. I can't be sure."

"Oh my God," she whispered. "Is there any way we can stop them from getting in? From getting to us?"

"I don't think so," Shane answered. "Our best bet maybe my knuckledusters, but I wanted to poke around the tools and see if there's anything which could help."

"Okay," Courtney said, standing up. "Let's look."

Shane got to his feet and walked with her to the pile of equipment left behind by the unfortunate Mike Puller.

Most of what they found was fairly common. Nail gun, compressor, and nails by the thousands. For nearly twenty minutes they moved aside the different tools and supplies.

"Look at this, Shane," Courtney said.

"What's that, Cort?" Shane said, glancing over.

Beneath a pile of boards was an old, short bookcase. On it was a few stacks of books and the old photo albums the Victorians had favored. Shane walked over, squatted down, and looked at the volumes.

Most of the titles dealt with ships, maritime law, and coastal soundings. Three of the books were ledgers, taller and thinner than the others and with the marbled boards so common for the time. Two of the leather bound books were photograph albums, each equipped with a pair of brass hinges and matched clasps to keep the covers closed.

Courtney took one of the albums and sat back, opening it while Shane slipped one of the ledgers off of the shelf. He stood up and opened the book carefully. It smelled of the sea, and old, dry paper. The ruled green, horizontal lines, bisected by double red lines on either margin, were filled with neat, orderly sentences.

It's a journal, Shane realized. The first entry was September 9th, 1881.

"Oh Jesus Christ, Shane," Courtney whispered. She held the album up for him to see.

A glance at the sepia toned image showed a pair of children. Twin boys, each dressed in short pants and ruffled shirts. Between them was a woman, dressed in a long, dark dress, eyes closed and propped up in a casket between them.

Mother, was written beneath the photograph.

Shane turned over several of the heavy pages. Each page had a single photo. The others in the images were all alive. He opened the album to the center and stiffened.

"Cort," he said softly, handing it back to her.

She took it, looked at the photo it had been left open to, and quickly closed the album. Courtney's lips were pressed tightly together, and she swallowed several times before she managed to say, "Dorothy."

Shane nodded.

Courtney put the album back on the shelf. She took a deep breath, let it out slowly, and then asked, "What have you got there?"

"Someone's journal," he replied.

"Whose?"

"I don't know," Shane said. He looked at the front-end paper and found only a stamp for a bookstore in Concord, New Hampshire. At the end of the book, on the last page, he saw a name and an address. He read them both out loud,

"'*Dorothy Miller, Squirrel Island Lighthouse, Maine.*'"

"Shane," Courtney said, concern heavy in her voice.

"Yes?" he asked, closing and tucking the book beneath his arm.

"Why are you smiling?"

Shane hadn't realized he had been. As soon as she pointed it out, his smile spread into a grin. "This is what I need."

"Why?" Courtney asked.

"It'll tell me what I need to know–" he began, but a pounding on the door cut him off.

His heart thudded in his chest, and he handed the book to Courtney.

"Stay behind me," he said.

She slipped behind him, resting a small hand on his back.

The hammering on the door continued.

"Who is it?" Shane called out.

The knocking stopped.

"It's Scott."

"What's going on, Scott?" Shane asked calmly.

"I'd like to come in," the young man replied.

"I don't know about that," Shane said.

He doesn't believe he's dead, Shane thought. *He doesn't believe he can just come in.*

"Why not?" Scott asked, a confused tone in his voice.

"I'm pretty sure you're dead, kid," Shane answered.

Scott hesitated before he said, "No, I'm not."

"Think about it for a while," Shane said, kindly, "and then get back to me in the morning."

"What if they come for me?" Scott said.

"They already did."

"I'm not dead," Scott said softly, his voice barely audible through the door.

Sadness crept up into Shane's heart, and he said, "You are, Scott. I'm sorry, kid."

A plaintive wail ripped through the lighthouse. Silence followed, and after several minutes, Courtney put her head against Shane's back and cried.

Shane turned around, took her into his arms, and guided her to the wall. They sat down, and Shane comforted her as best he could.

Chapter 28: Whiskey and Bad Decisions

George was drunker than he had been in a long time. It helped him forget about Vic and Eric. And the blonde cougar on his arm aided as well.

She kept him steady and on his feet as they wandered down Main Street towards the marina. The touch of her hand on his arm, the power of her scent, the alcohol he had consumed, all of it made him giddy. Continuing on down the road, she guided him, gently but firmly.

"What's your name again?" George asked, impressed at how little his words slurred as he spoke.

She gave him a wink. "Mystery."

"'Mystery?'" George repeated, chuckling. "That's a hell of a handle. Why'd your parents name you that?"

Mystery laughed, shook her head and told him, "You are a funny man when you drink, George."

He straightened up with the compliment. *Nobody's told me I was funny before. I must be, though. Mystery's the best.*

Ahead of them, George caught sight of the gate to the marina. Powerful street lights illuminated the newly painted white boards and the salty smell of the Atlantic, always strong, hammered through his drunken nose. The rich, intoxicating scent of the salt water made him grin.

"What's the smile for?" Mystery asked.

"The ocean," George said. "I love it. Always have."

"Do you work it?" she asked.

George shook his head and nearly knocked himself over, but Mystery's surprisingly strong grip kept him from falling.

"Nah," he said, "I'm in construction. You know. Hammer. Nails."

"Hammer? Nails?" She leaned in and whispered into his ear, her breath hot against him. "Sounds suggestive, George. Where's this boat of yours?"

"Right this way, sweetheart," he answered, wobbling as they

reached the gate and opened it.

The small gatehouse, tucked off to the right and in a deep shadow, suddenly glowed with light.

Both George and Mystery stopped, the woman turning her head away and putting a hand up to block the harsh glare which threatened to blind them both.

George was too drunk look away. He merely squeezed his eyes shut.

The door hinges of the gatehouse screamed as it was opened.

"George?" Dell Fort called out. "Is that you?"

"It is," George snapped. "Turn the damned light out, Dell."

A moment later, the partial darkness returned, and George opened his eyes.

"Christ, George," Dell said angrily, "it's after two! Why the hell aren't you at home?"

Dell's sentence ended when he stepped closer and saw Mystery on George's arm, her head still turned away.

"Ah, hell," Dell muttered. "Go on in. Keep it quiet, though, alright? The McCormicks are in their boat. Those old farts complain if someone answers a phone call after nightfall."

"You got it, Dell," George said, grinning.

Dell waved them on and turned away.

Mystery pulled George close and murmured, "I almost thought our night was ruined."

A thrill raced through George, and he breathed heavy as he answered, "No one's ruining it. I'll take her out, away from shore. McCormicks won't complain then."

"I was thinking the same," she said softly.

George staggered down the pier towards *Terminal Fleet*, his steps misguided by equal parts of alcohol and lust. Mystery's hold on his arm quickened his pace.

Chapter 29: Close to Dawn

Courtney awoke, hungry and miserable. She lifted her head off of Shane's lap and sat up. He closed the ledger he was reading and smiled softly at her.

"How are you feeling?" he asked her.

"Terrible," she replied. She could smell whiskey and cigarettes, sweat and concern, which she found strangely comforting.

"Understood," Shane said. He picked up a bottle of water and passed it over to her. "Rinse and spit out the first mouthful. The rest will taste better."

"Spit where?" she asked, opening the bottle.

He grinned. "Anywhere you like, Cort. We won't be here much longer, one way or the other."

A chill raced through her at his words. She did as he said with the water, and found he was right. She drank all of the water quickly.

"You've figured a way out?" she said softly. "Or are we out of luck?"

"A way to stop Dorothy, and the others," he said. "And I'll be smashing the absolute hell out of the lantern if I can't do what I'm planning."

"How are you going to stop her?" Courtney asked.

Shane lifted up the ledger. "With this. All three of them, actually. Everything she was, she wrote in here. And when she was afraid someone might read her words, she wrote Latin. She was a smart woman. Angry, but smart."

"You read Latin?" Courtney asked, surprised.

"Yup," Shane said, smiling. "Lots of other languages too. But what she wrote in Latin, is the key to the power over her."

"What do you mean?" Courtney asked.

"Here," Shane said, opening the ledger up. He flipped through several pages, stopped and said, "Let me read this to you,

"We have been here too long. Far too long. Ione has

95

left us. The willful girl, and I doubt I shall see my eldest daughter again soon. This leaves me with the task of caring for my beastly husband and the remainder of our wretched children. My father will not survive long. He will move on to the next world, either by God's will or by my hands."

A painful terror gripped Courtney's empty stomach, and she whispered, "She planned her father's death?"

"His, and the death of her children. Her husband as well," Shane said. "She hid the bodies. Both to avoid punishment and out of shame. There's more. Revelations about past sins, and those she wished to commit. By hiding them from all others, even in her private thoughts, she's shown there is a power over her through them."

"What are you going to do?" Courtney said.

"Find her and bind her to the physical world," Shane said.

"What then?" Courtney asked.

"I'll break her," Shane said. "Break her and cast her to Hell, because I'm pretty sure she's headed there when all is said and done."

He set the ledger down, grabbed an MRE, and opened it, passing it over to her. She dumped it out onto the floor in front of her, spotted a package of crackers and another of peanut butter.

"Breakfast of champions?" she asked tiredly.

"You've no idea, Cort," Shane said, smiling. "I ate those damned things for years, out in the field. And when you're hungry, and you can't stand the sight of them, you still choke it down."

She tore open the peanut butter, ate some of it from the small container, and then said, "You're a strange man."

"Me?" he asked, surprised.

"Yes, you," she said. "Here you are, retired military and ghost hunter, and you read Latin."

"More than just Latin," he said in a voice suddenly tired and worn.

"Really?" she said, opening the crackers. "What else?"

"French, Spanish, Portuguese, Russian, Greek, German," Shane said. "And a whole lot more than that."

"How can you read all of those?" she asked, surprised.

"Read, write, and speak," Shane said. "I don't know how, exactly. Languages are easy. I hear it, and I can speak it. And if I can read it, then I can write it."

"That's amazing," Courtney said. "What do you for work? I mean, you can't be a full-time ghost hunter, right?"

"Right," Shane said, smiling. "I'm a freelance translator. Plus, I have my pension from the Marine Corps, in the end, so everything's working out pretty well. Even this."

"What do you mean?" Courtney said, her heart fluttering.

"I got to meet you," Shane said softly. "I wish there wasn't so much death around us, but I'm pleased we met. Exceptionally pleased."

"Me too," Courtney said, and she took out a cracker to eat, her smile too big to hide.

Chapter 30: Seeing the Sunrise over the Atlantic

George felt as though a thousand little fists were hammering against his head. His mouth was painfully dry, and when he tried to move, he found he couldn't. He cracked open an eye, but the sun was breaking the horizon, filling the Atlantic with its powerful light.

I'm on the boat, he realized dully.

He tried to move again and was able to roll over onto his back. Blinking he tried to focus, and he saw he was on the deck. In the chair so recently occupied by Vic, sat Mystery.

Even after sleeping in her clothes, and on board a Boston Whaler, she was stunning. She sat with her legs crossed delicately and sipping from a bottle of water. When she saw he was awake, she adjusted her mirrored sunglasses and smiled at him with full, red lips.

"Good morning, George," she said pleasantly.

"Morning," he replied grumpily. In spite of his efforts to sit up, he couldn't. Something held him back. *I'm so hung over.*

"You, my fine, fat friend," she said, grinning, "can drink a lot of whiskey. I was impressed. I thought for certain I'd have to roll you out to your boat, but you made it."

George closed his eyes. Licked his lips, swallowed once to try and moisten his throat, and then said, "Where are we?"

"We are windward of Squirrel Island, looking at the back of the lighthouse and the keeper's house," she replied.

George stiffened and kept his eyes shut. "You're kidding, right?"

"Not at all," Mystery said happily.

"Why the hell did I bring us out here?" he asked with a groan.

"You didn't," she said. "I did."

George opened his eyes and looked at the woman. "Why, in God's name, would you do that?"

"Afraid, are you?" she asked, her voice taking on a dangerous calm.

"No," George lied.

"Of course, you are," she said softly. "You left your friends out here to die. You know it."

Did I talk when I was drunk? he thought frantically. *Good God, what did I say?*

His panic must have shown because Mystery laughed, a pleased and joyous sound.

"No, you fat, cowardly drunk," she said, smiling. "You said nothing. Well, at least not about the lighthouse. No, not a word. But I know."

Terror took over him. "I know all about your abandonment of your two friends," she said. "I agree, they were stupid not to have gotten back into your boat. Your own effort, perhaps, should have been greater, to get them to go away with you. And, failing to do so, you should have remained."

Her face went hard as she leaned forward. "You should have remained. You have caused me a great deal of inconvenience, *George*, and you shall suffer for it."

"I didn't do anything," he said, his voice was hoarse with fear.

"Liar," Mystery said, lounging back in the chair. "Liar, liar, liar. You'll get yours, though, George. You will indeed. I expect her to be here soon. Very soon."

"Who?" George whispered.

"My great-grandmother," the woman said sweetly. She adjusted her sunglasses, tilted her head back slightly and said, "Watching the sun rise over the Atlantic is always an occasion to treasure. Always."

George writhed on the deck, trying to get up.

"Give it up," she said, yawning. "I've trussed you up like a Thanksgiving turkey. You won't be going anywhere. Not until she arrives and decides what to do with you."

"What will she do with me?" George whispered.

"If you're lucky," Mystery said, smiling softly, "you'll drown and be on your way."

"And if I'm not?"

"If you're not," she said, the smile fading away, "you'll drown and be here until the end of time."

Chapter 31: Risking a Look

Shane stank.

His body smelled of old sweat and fear. Although he had managed to clean up a little with some wet-wipes he had brought along, it hadn't made much of a difference.

She doesn't smell, he thought, looking at Courtney.

He pulled out a flameless heater from an MRE and prepped a bag for coffee.

"You look like you know what you're doing," Courtney said, coming over and sitting down next to him.

"Looks are deceiving," he said with a grin. She had been crying again earlier, but it was to be expected.

I'll worry if she doesn't cry, he thought.

"Not in your case," she said confidently. "Everything you are is right out front, isn't it?"

Shane could tell the question was rhetorical, but he nodded in agreement anyway. "I don't see a need to hide anything. Not anymore. I played things pretty close to the vest for a long time. Can't really tell your friends the house you lived in killed your parents."

Her eyes widened, and she said softly, "Oh my God, I'm so sorry."

"Don't be," Shane said, sighing, "it was a long time ago."

He shook the bag with the coffee in it and added water to the flameless heater's bag. Once the chemicals in the heater reacted, he slipped both the containers into a cardboard sleeve, propped them up against the wall at an angle, and relaxed a little more.

"Did you sleep at all?" Courtney asked.

"A little, here and there," he said.

"How much is a little?"

"Maybe an hour altogether," Shane said. He tried not to think about how tired he felt.

"Do you want to sleep now?" she asked.

"No," he said, shaking his head. "It would only make it worse.

Better to stay up until everything is done."

"What do you want to do after the coffee?" Courtney said, glancing over at the door.

"Take a walk," Shane replied. "I want to see if we can find some more iron somewhere."

"Where would we find iron?"

"We'll take a quick look around the house," Shane said. "Then we'll go down by the pier. We'll do it together, though. They may be a little cautious around me, and we'll have to work with what we have."

"Yeah," Courtney said, "I'm not leaving your side, Shane."

"Glad to hear it," he said, smiling. "Coffee's about ready. Want some?"

"God yes," she said, sighing.

Shane poured the brew out into their sole cup and handed it to her.

"Thanks." She blew on it to cool it down, took a sip, and winced. "Damn, that's strong."

"We need it to be," Shane said. "Sometimes, when we were out in the field, and we were all jonesing for a caffeine fix, we'd take the instant coffee from the MREs and use the crystals like they were chew."

"I have no idea what that means," she said, grinning.

"You know, chewing tobacco?" Shane asked. When she nodded, he said, "Well, we would stick a pinch of the instant between our gum and cheek. Sort of suck the caffeine out of it."

"Sounds absolutely disgusting," Courtney said.

"It was," Shane said, smiling as he remembered. "But you do what you need to do."

"And what we need to do today is find iron?" she said.

"If we can," Shane said, nodding.

"What if we can't?"

"Hope like hell that we can," Shane said with a shrug of his shoulders.

Together they drank the coffee, ate some less-than-appealing breakfast, and got ready for the day. Shane gave Courtney one of his clean t-shirts to wear and politely turned his back while she changed. She extended him the same courtesy while he switched out all of his clothes.

"Ready?" Shane asked her, his hand on the latch.

She nodded.

"Remember, we go everywhere together."

"Got it," Courtney said grimly.

"Okay."

Shane took a deep breath and opened the door. The sun had come up only a short time before, and the wind was stronger than it had been. The waves were in a frenzy, the whitecaps mad as they danced along the breadth of water between the mainland and the island. The pier and the stones suffered beneath each wave.

Shane stood still and looked out at the island.

He saw nothing out of place. No one walking around, no ghosts waiting for them.

"Alright," he said, glancing back at Courtney.

His eyes widened.

What remained of Scott stood behind her, and smiled at Shane.

Chapter 32: In for Rough Weather

The Boston Whaler pitched and rolled with the ocean. The waves were getting larger, and George could see them from his position on the deck.

She'll be swamped soon, George thought, depressed.

The mystery woman was either unaware of the danger or didn't care. She continued to lounge in her seat. He could see the knuckles on her hands whiten as the boat rose up, and then followed the curve of a wave down.

"How are you feeling, George?" she asked pleasantly, no hint of concern in her voice.

He didn't respond.

"Oh, you don't want to talk now?" she said, laughing. "I couldn't get you to shut up last night. The promises you made."

George kept his comments to himself. He was afraid. Not of her, but of whatever was coming from the island for him. He had no doubt about it. Somewhere, something was on its way.

And I'm going to die, he thought.

Mystery stood up suddenly, a triumphant smile on her face. She retained her balance and poise as the boat rolled with the waves.

"Great Mother," she said respectfully, taking off her sunglasses.

Without knowing why George twisted to see who the woman spoke to.

A middle-aged woman, her face harsh and severe, had arrived, somehow. Her hands were clasped loosely together in front of her, and she looked disdainfully at George.

George's heart lost all sense of rhythm, beating erratically as he looked through the new arrival. The edges of her body had no clear sense of definition, and the world beyond was disturbed, as though by a gossamer curtain.

George struggled as panic flooded him, and his frantic efforts brought a cold smile to the Great Mother's face.

"His fear is palpable," the new arrival said. "You've done well, girl. Exceptionally so. Soon we'll have enough to put the lighthouse to right."

"Thank you, Great Mother," Mystery replied, a sense of awe in her voice. "Do you require more?"

"A few. Just a few."

George continued to struggle, his hands and feet numb from hours of being bound. All of his attempts were useless. Finally, he let out a cry and closed his eyes as he gave up.

"Bring him to the island," the Great Mother said. "I must put the newest of the help through their paces."

The Whaler's engine started up, and George felt the boat begin to move. He risked a look and opened an eye. He saw Mystery at the helm, her back was to him.

"I'm sorry, George," she said over her shoulder, and there was no true note of sympathy or apology in her voice. "You will not be drowned today. Something worse, I'm sure, but at least you won't be drowned."

George shuddered.

I'd rather drown, he thought miserably. *Dear God, please kill me now.*

God didn't answer, and George began to weep.

Chapter 33: Uninvited and Unwanted

Shane closed the door carefully, never taking his eyes off of Scott. Or rather the horror which had been Scott. The dead had mangled the young man. His clothes were gone, but he wasn't naked. It was worse.

Scott was nothing more than a bloody sketch of what he had been prior to his death. His eyes were gone. Destroyed sockets seemed to stare at Shane. He had been flayed, all of the muscles laid bare for the world to see. Teeth were broken, shattered remnants of what they had been. Each finger was a twisted horror, a nightmare idea of what the digits should be.

What did they do with the body? Shane wondered. *Did they drag it down into the ocean after? Did they stuff it down amongst the rocks for the crabs and fish to eat?*

"Why'd you close the door?" Courtney asked, confused. "I thought we were going out."

"We will be," Shane said, keeping his eyes on Scott as he answered her. "Cort, do you trust me?"

"Yes," she said, frowning.

"I'm going to tell you to do something, and I need you to do it exactly as I say. Do you understand?" Shane asked.

She nodded, fear replacing the confusion.

"Good. Without looking around, I want you to sidestep to your right and never take your eyes off of me. When you reach the wall, sit down, close your eyes, and keep them that way until I tell you to open them."

He saw her swallow nervously, but she did as she was told. Shane kept his attention fixed on Scott. Finally, he said, "How are you, Scott?"

The destroyed visage focused on him, and the mouth moved as Scott said, "I won't lie, Shane. I have been a *whole* lot better."

"Kind of figured that out," Shane said. "Are you in pain?"

"No," Scott answered. "Got to tell you, it wasn't pleasant."

"I don't imagine it was."

"Thanks for opening the door, by the way," Scott said cheerfully. "For some reason, I couldn't get through it last night."

"Why are you here?" Shane asked.

"I've come for the little whore," Scott said, laughing. "Dorothy wants you. Wants you all to herself. And, from what I hear, she's going to make an *example* out of you. I'm really looking forward to watching that."

There was no more joy in Scott's voice, only hatred.

"Oh yes," the young man said softly, "I will enjoy watching you suffer. Watching you die. There's been some talk of keeping you on, but I hope she won't. I hope she sends your rotten soul straight to Hell."

"She might," Shane said. "You really can't rule anything out."

"No, you can't," Scott said, nodding in agreement. "Anyway, I've come to get Courtney."

When Scott turned his head to look at her with eyes no longer there, Shane attacked. He threw himself across the short distance which separated him from Scott. He brought the knuckledusters smashing down on Scott.

The young man screamed a sound of pure rage which instantly gave Shane a headache. Scott disappeared, and Shane lost his balance, tripped, and slammed into the thick wall of the Lighthouse. He knocked over some of the equipment but caught himself before he fell.

"Courtney," Shane said, standing up and looking at her. "He's gone now."

She opened her eyes, anger and fear combined within them. She got to her feet and went to Shane. Her body shook, her face was pale, but she exuded strength.

"Where did he go?" she asked.

"To wherever they hid his body, I'm assuming," Shane said, flexing his hands and letting out a deep, shuddering breath.

"I need something to protect myself with," Courtney said. "I need it now."

Shane nodded his agreement. He turned his attention to the lighthouse door. The latch was iron. The hinges were iron.

He went to a tool bag set on the floor by the bookcase.

"Are we going to go into the house to look?" Courtney asked.

"No," Shane said, pulling the bag open and rummaging through it. "Look at the door."

"What about it?"

"The hinges, the handle. Hell, even the straps on the boards, they're all made of iron," Shane said, shaking his head at his own ignorance. He took a pry-bar and a two-pound sledge out of the bag. He carried both over to the door and looked at the hinges.

"Pinions," he said, pointing at them.

Courtney's smile was cold and knowing. "They'll pop right out."

"Yup," he said. He fit the edge of the pry bar beneath the lip of the pin on the first hinge and banged it out. He did the same with the other two hinges, handing all three of the pins to Courtney. Then with the door held in place only by the latch and luck, he put the tools down and took the door out of the frame. He set it against the inner wall and examined it.

The wood was old but still strong.

This'll take some work, he sighed.

"What's wrong?" Courtney asked.

"Nothing," Shane said, smiling at her. "Hold onto those pins, alright?"

"Sure," she said. "Are we putting the door back up?"

"No," Shane said, shaking his head. "I'm going to get one of these hinges off, try to make you a club of some sort."

Courtney nodded. She examined the pins and then asked, "So, think these would work too?"

"In a pinch," he replied. "I'd rather you have something with a little more reach. I don't think they're going to come at us individually. They'll probably swarm. Dorothy's not stupid, she'll have seen we have at least a little iron. That'll keep her about as honest as possible. Which isn't much."

"No," Courtney said bitterly, "it's not."

"Alright," Shane said, picking up the sledge. "It's going to get loud."

Courtney smirked. "That's how I like it."

Shane laughed, caught off guard. "Okay, then. Sounds good to me."

He lifted the sledge and brought it down hard on the door.

Chapter 34: The Forecast

With her morning run finished, Marie was in her den. She was stretching and cooling down as the news played out on the small television. The forecast was calling for high winds, possible rain, and thunderstorms, with a high-wave warning for the coastal communities.

She frowned as she straightened up. *It's been too long without any word from him. Or from Amy about him,* Marie thought.

Calm down, she told herself. *Amy said she'd let you know as soon as she heard from him.*

You could always call her. There is rough weather coming in.

Marie nodded to herself, went to her coffee table, and picked up her phone. She dialed Amy's number, but after three rings, it went to voicemail. Marie left a message asking her cousin to call back.

Still holding her phone, Marie went and sat down on the edge of her couch. She turned up the volume on the television.

A yacht had been found drifting off the coast of Maine. The anchor line had snapped, and the Coast Guard was out looking for the crew. No one had been reported missing, but the yacht had left its berth three days earlier. According to the news report, the boat had been spotted anchored close to Squirrel Island, but that had been the last reported sighting.

Marie frowned.

An abandoned yacht, last seen near Squirrel Island. Where Shane Ryan is investigating the ghostly connection to a suicide.

Jesus Christ, she thought, *Amy better get back to me soon, or I'll be going up there myself.*

The idea of being on the ocean again churned her stomach.

I can't leave him out there. And what if the crew is there, too?

Marie turned off the television, got up, and went towards the bedroom. She needed to shower and get to work. In her head, she calculated how long it might take to charter a boat out to the Squirrel Island Lighthouse.

Chapter 35: An Unexpected Guest

The weapon was ugly. A length of board cut down to roughly two feet. One end was wrapped tightly with strips of one of Shane's t-shirts. The head of the bludgeon was a pair of hinges, beaten and battered into shape.

"Swing it," Shane said, stepping back after he had handed it to Courtney.

The muscles in her forearms stood out as she lifted it up into the batter's position. She set her feet, her mouth set grimly. She took a deep breath and gave a swing that made Shane's eyes widen with appreciation.

"Damn," Shane said, chuckling. "You would have hit it out of the park."

She winked at him, lowering the weapon. "Played softball in high school, and at Rivier University in New Hampshire."

"It shows," Shane said. "How does it feel, though?"

"Rough," she said. "Wouldn't want to try and hit a ball with it, but I think I can crush anything that steps up to me."

"Good. You've got the pins still, too?"

She nodded. "Back pocket."

"Okay, keep them there. If you lose the cudgel, use those. One in each hand," he said.

"Got it."

He picked up the last item he had made. It was the third hinge, bent into a crescent shape. He had threaded strips of cloth through the nail holes and made a rough pair of knuckledusters for his left hand.

"So," Courtney started to say, and then she stopped. She pointed out the open doorway and Shane turned to look.

A boat was at the pier.

Is it the same boat from yesterday? Shane wondered dazedly. *Did he come back for his friends?*

"Should we go down there?" Courtney said cautiously. "It's the same boat as yesterday."

"Is it?" Shane asked.

Courtney nodded. "*Terminal Fleet.* I saw the name."

He caught sight of a woman wearing sunglasses and a large hat, her blonde hair pulled into a ponytail. She was also wearing what looked like an oversized man's sweatshirt. For a moment, she ducked down, and when she came back up, she was dragging a man. A man whose hands and legs were bound behind his back. She pushed him over the side of the boat, and Shane heard his body thump on the wood of the pier.

"Oh Goddamn," Courtney hissed. "They'll kill him."

Shane nodded and led the way out of the lighthouse. With Courtney at his side, he jogged down, keeping an eye out for the dead. Inwardly he groaned as the boat's engine shifted gears and it peeled away from the pier.

"Shane," Courtney said.

He turned partially and saw Mike Puller. The man closed in on them, and when he was close enough, Courtney swung.

Mike shrieked as the head of the cudgel connected, the man vanished.

Courtney grinned. "It works."

They picked up their pace, and soon their feet were pounding on the pier. When they reached the bound man, Shane dropped to a knee, took out his work knife, and flicked it open with one hand. The stranger's arms and legs were zip-tied, and Shane cut them away quickly.

The man whimpered, rolled onto his side, and looked up at Shane.

"We're going to die," the stranger whispered.

"That's a given," Shane replied. "But let's make sure it's not today."

He helped the man to his feet, the stranger grimacing. Shane let the man lean on him, and he said, "Ready, Cort?"

She nodded and led the way back to the lighthouse.

Thankfully, they were left alone.

Chapter 36: At the Marina

Dell Fort was tired and in a decidedly bad mood.

Frankie McCrory had called in sick for the first shift, which meant Dell had to cover for him.

I'm so tired, Dell thought, dumping three packets of sugar into his fresh coffee. He added cream, put the container back into the mini-fridge in the gatehouse, and glared out the front window. He had the gates unlocked and open. A few of the natives had been in to check on their boats and there were too many of the summer folk for his liking.

They pay the bills, Dell, he reminded himself. With a sigh, he took a drink, winced at how hot it was, and put his mug down. Movement caught his attention, and he looked down at the end of the marina. George Fallon's new Boston Whaler, *Terminal Fleet,* was coasting into its berth.

Dell smirked. George had been out all night with his lady friend. Dell waited, hoping to catch sight of her.

"Dell!"

The sharp, waspish voice of Mr. Webb forced Dell to turn away from Fallon's boat and look out the front window. Mr. Webb, gangly and unkempt, per usual, held up his monthly bill.

"What is it, Mr. Webb?" Dell asked. Long ago, he had given up trying to be polite to the man. Webb was a colossal pain, no matter how nice Dell was.

"You raised the berthing fees again," Mr. Webb snapped.

"Mr. Webb," Dell said patiently, "I didn't do anything of the sort. The Marina Association did, though. They raised the berthing fees for everyone. Not just you."

"I didn't think it was just me," Mr. Webb said. "And I know it's you."

Oh, Jesus, Dell thought, *why the hell did Frankie have to call in sick today?*

"Mr. Webb," Dell said, "if you'd like to lodge a complaint you'd be better off writing a letter or sending an email."

"Don't you tell me what to do, Dell Fort!" Mr. Webb yelled, his voice rising to nearly a shriek. He shook the bill at Dell, turned around, and stomped off to the beat-up Ford station wagon he drove. Dell watched as black smoke billowed out of the car's exhaust and Mr. Webb puttered out of the parking lot.

The man has more money than God, and he complains because the Association raised his berthing fee by ten dollars a month, Dell thought.

His inner monologue was interrupted by another person, but this one came from the pier. It was a woman, her blonde hair pulled back in a messy ponytail and a large, tan fisherman's cap on her head. She wore mirrored sunglasses and a dark blue sweatshirt that was way too big for her. The hem of the shirt hung down to the mid-thigh of her khaki capris. Her hands were tucked into the front pocket of the sweatshirt.

When she passed by the gatehouse, Dell saw "Fallon Construction" in white letters on the back of the pullover.

Dell shook his head as she passed through the parking lot and up Marion Street. He glanced up the marina, but he didn't see any movement on board the Boston Whaler.

Must have been one hell of a night, Dell thought. He took up his coffee, took a sip, and winced.

Still too damned hot.

Chapter 37: At Squirrel Island

The man's name was George Fallon, and he was scared to death.

With good reason, too, Shane thought.

Courtney sat beside Shane, and George was across from them. He had deep marks on his wrists from the zip-ties. He had drunk nearly a gallon of water, and he constantly looked out of the open doorway.

"You said there's wood around here?" George said finally.

Shane nodded. "Round the back of the house, there's a pile of lumber for the construction work."

"Yeah," George said. "Would make sense. Mike wouldn't have rented a boat to go back and forth each day. Would have cut into his profits."

"Why are you asking about wood?" Courtney asked.

"I'm in construction," George answered. "All of Mike's tools are in here. Lumber's out back. I can build a door."

"It won't do much good," Courtney said. "Doors and walls don't stop them."

George's shoulders slumped, and he sighed unhappily.

"Who was the woman?" Shane asked. "The one who dumped you here and stole your boat?"

"Don't know," George said. "Met her in a bar last night; thought my luck was changing, especially after what happened here. We got drunk, she asked me for a ride on the boat, and I said yes."

"But why did she bring you here?" Shane asked.

"She said her great-grandmother was upset that I had gotten away," George said, his voice dropping to a whisper. "They're supposed to kill me."

Shane stiffened. "Her great-grandmother?"

George nodded.

"What did the woman look like?" Shane asked.

"You saw her," George said.

Shane shook his head. "Not really. Tell me."

George described her. "Attractive, blonde, tanned. Good walk, great laugh."

"How old?" Shane asked, his voice tightening.

"Forties, maybe?" George said. "Can't really remember too well, right now."

Shane stood up, anger pulsing through him. He walked over to the tools, picked up the two-pound sledge, and went to the stairs.

"Shane," Courtney said, "what are you doing?"

"I'm going to go smash the lantern," he said, starting up the steps.

"Why?" she said. "I thought we were going to wait and see if they were coming for you today."

"They're not," Shane said.

"How do you know?" Courtney asked.

Shane paused and looked at her.

"I know," he said angrily, "because the woman that dumped George on the island is the same one who hired me in the first place. No help is coming, Courtney. Not from her."

Gripping the handle of the sledgehammer tightly, Shane made his way up the top of the lighthouse.

Chapter 38: Reassurances

Marie Lafontaine looked at the ID on her phone when it rang and saw it was Amy.

"Hello?"

"Hey, cousin!" Amy said cheerfully. "I'm sorry I didn't answer the phone when you called. The damned thing never even rang."

"Everything alright with it?" Marie asked, leaning back in her chair and closing the file she had been working on.

"Yes," Amy answered. "It's Squirrel Island. The reception is terrible."

"What's going on out there? How's Shane?"

"He's looking devilishly handsome," Amy said, laughing. "I didn't think a man could be completely bald and still be attractive, but he is."

Marie shook her head and rolled her eyes at her cousin's antics. "You've always been too much, Amy."

"Says you," Amy said cheerfully. "Anyway, your fine-looking friend, Mr. Ryan, is not only rooting out the problem of the ghost but doing some fine construction work as well."

"That's a relief to hear," Marie said, and she meant it. She felt a weight slip off of her shoulders. "I was afraid I'd sent him into something he couldn't handle."

"Nonsense," Amy said. "He's a strapping young man."

Marie laughed. "Amy, he's as old as we are."

"You wouldn't know it by looking at him."

Marie sighed. "Cousin, you're too much. Anyway, so he's doing okay, then?"

"More than okay," Amy replied. In a serious tone she said, "Marie, I'll let you know if anything goes wrong. But he's doing well. He's a little upset about not having an internet connection, but other than that, everything is going exactly as planned."

"I'm glad to hear it," Marie said. "When are you picking him up again?"

"Two more days," Amy said. "He said everything should be wrapped up by then. Do you want to meet me here and we'll pick him up together?"

"Yes, I'd like that," Marie said.

"Then it's set," Amy said. "I'll talk to you tomorrow, and we'll make all the plans."

"Great."

They ended the call, and Marie returned to her work. She whistled to herself and felt far better than she had before.

Chapter 39: Calling for Help

Shane was angry.

A deep, chilling anger which he nursed and cared for. He ground his teeth and made his way to the top of the lighthouse. He switched the two-pound sledgehammer from his left hand to his right, the grip awkward with the protection he wore on his hands.

Can't risk taking it off, he thought, squeezing the wooden shaft of the tool tightly. *Too dangerous.*

When he had reached the lantern, he examined it closely.

So many people saved by such a simple idea, Shane thought. He raised the sledge and swung it with all of his strength. The lens shattered easily, reflective material exploding outward from the force of the blow. Shane breathed deeply, then struck it twice more.

He brushed fragments of glass off of himself, frowning at tiny nicks and scratches on his arms from the flying debris. Still holding tightly onto the sledgehammer, Shane went down and joined Courtney and George. Shane dropped the tool onto the floor, kicked a few shards away, and sat down next to Courtney.

"What the hell did you do that for?" George asked, confused.

"Coast Guard must monitor the lighthouses, right?" Shane said.

George nodded. "Yeah. They monitor all of them. It's a federal offense to mess around with them."

"Good," Shane said. "It's the only chance we have for getting off this island alive."

Comprehension brightened George's eyes. "They'll send a boat out to see what happened."

Shane nodded.

"Still, you're probably going to end up doing some time for the vandalism," George said, grinning.

Shane smiled. "More than happy to. That means I'll be alive."

"Don't worry," Courtney said, reaching out and taking his hand. "I'll come and visit."

"Fair enough," Shane said. "That alone, makes it all worthwhile."

"Ahoy the lighthouse!" a voice called from outside.

Shane let go of Courtney's hand and quickly stood up. Two long strides carried him to the open doorway, and he looked for the speaker.

Clark, the lighthouse keeper, stood a short distance down the path. Dane was beside him, a terrified expression on his face. Both men were difficult to see in the bright morning light.

"Mr. Noyes," Shane called back. "What can I do for you?"

"You can first let me compliment you on your manners, my Marine," Clark said cheerfully. "Ever polite you are. Well done, sir."

Shane inclined his head slightly. "Many thanks. Now, back to my question, if you will."

"Ah, yes," Clark said, nodding. "Business. My wife, Dorothy, well she has laid a claim on the man who has come to you this morning. A relative of ours brought him here specifically for my wife. You've no right to keep him from her."

"I have every right," Shane said coldly.

"You'll not send him out, then?" Clark asked, frowning.

"No," Shane said, shaking his head.

Behind him, Shane heard George let out a shuddering breath.

"Anything else, Mr. Noyes?" Shane asked.

"Yes," Clark said, his voice going cold, anger creeping into it. "I see you went ahead and broke my light."

"I did."

"Will you be repairing it?" Clark demanded.

"Of course, I will see it is repaired when I reach the mainland," Shane answered.

"Damn your eyes!" Clark snarled, taking a step forward even as Dane shrank back. "Do you have any idea of the danger you're putting those ships and crews in?"

"I do," Shane said.

"You're a monster," Clark hissed.

Shane laughed, surprised at the comment. "Ah, Mr. Noyes, at least I didn't condemn a boy to an eternity of servitude to care for a flashlight."

"It's a lighthouse, you twit," Clark said, his voice low and thick with anger. "And it needs to be cared for."

"It will be," Shane said, all humor gone. "You'd best run along to your mistress now, Mr. Clark. Go be about her business since she won't let you be about yours."

"My mistress has plans for you, Shane Ryan. She will teach you to have a civil tongue, or she will take it out." Clark turned and walked to the keeper's house, Dane following quickly behind him. Once they had disappeared into the small home, Shane left the doorway and returned to his seat.

"They were dead," George said after a minute.

Shane nodded.

"The lighthouse keeper," Courtney hissed, her voice filled with both anger and bitterness, "and the others, they've murdered everyone."

"Shane," George said, his voice thin and fearful. "What's going to happen?"

"We're going to fight," Shane answered. "First, I need some more coffee. Then I need to read the rest of Dorothy's journals. I need to know more; I need to know her better."

"Who is she?" George asked. "And why the hell do you need to know her better?"

"She's the one in charge," Shane said. Courtney started to help him prepare the coffee. "I need to understand her better so I can figure out how to destroy her. Hey, we've got powdered cream and sugar from an MRE, if you want a cup of coffee."

Dazed, George nodded.

Shane whistled the Marine Corps hymn as he worked beside Courtney, her hand occasionally brushing his.

Chapter 40: Bad News

Amy pulled on an old t-shirt and a battered pair of shorts after she had taken a quick shower. She had washed off the stink of the bar, the sweat of George, and the dirty smell of the Marina. In the bathroom, she ran the hair-dryer and then unplugged it before she wandered tiredly out to her bed.

With an exaggerated sigh, she flopped down, adjusted the pillows and wondered if she would be able to get any sleep. She was excited.

Everything is nearly done, she thought, closing her eyes and smiling.

The locket on her chest suddenly felt like an ice-cube against her skin.

"Oh Christ!" she shouted, jumping up off of the bed pulling the chain up over her head. Pain screamed through her hand as she cast the locket onto the bed, the latch springing open and the bit of broken mirror, within the metal, started gleaming.

Dorothy appeared in the room, her dead face shrouded in a mask of silent rage.

"Great Mother," Amy whispered, backing up nervously and sitting down in the chair at her vanity.

"Child," Dorothy said, no affection or care in her voice. "I am displeased."

Panic wormed its way into Amy's heart. "What is it? What's wrong? What did I do?"

A small smile appeared on Dorothy's face. "You accept blame. And for that, you are forgiven. So few can do so."

A minor tremor of relief passed through Amy, and she whispered, "What have I done wrong?"

"You left too quickly," Dorothy said, the smile vanishing. "Shane and his young woman rescued the man you left for me. They are within the lighthouse. The keeper is in a rage for they have broken the light.

"And you know what shall happen without the light?" Dorothy

asked, her voice growing cold.

"Nothing," Amy whispered. "Nothing will happen."

Dorothy nodded. "I will continue to be bound to the island, restricted to these brief excursions. I will not have enough souls to thrust me forward, to release me. I *need* the dead. I do not believe I can stress this enough, Child."

"I know," Amy whispered. Then she frowned and said, "The light. Why would they break the light?"

Dorothy looked at her coldly. "What do you think will occur when the lighthouse does not shine this evening?"

"Oh God," Amy said in a small voice as she straightened up. She felt panic rise up within her throat.

I'm going to fail her! she thought frantically. *I can't fail her! I can't!*

"Someone will come," Amy moaned. "They'll be rescued!"

"Stop it, then!" Dorothy commanded. "This may be only a way for me to reach out and speak to you, but I promise, there are many other ways in which I can hurt you. And I will, in my own time."

Amy swallowed dryly, nodded and said softly, "I will, Great Mother."

Without a word or a gesture, Dorothy vanished. Amy's body trembled, and it took her a few minutes to gather up the courage to stand up and walk to her bed. Her hand shook as she picked up the locket and held it tightly in her palm.

The small piece of jewelry had passed through generations to her.

I will not fail you, Great Mother, Amy thought, closing the locket. It was no longer bitterly cold, only cool and comforting as she slipped it back over her neck. *The lighthouse will be restored, and we will be great keepers again.*

She climbed onto the bed, pulled a sheet over her, and sighed.

I've got a couple of hours, she thought. *Get some rest, then find the Coast Guard and have a little chat.*

She smiled, closed her eyes, and let herself search for sleep.

Chapter 41: Seeking the Way

I have played at this game for far too long. Five children with that witless oaf. The only child worth a damn gone to the mainland. And who can blame her? Certainly not I. And my hated father, the proverbial albatross about my neck. Would that he had gone down with his ship off the Grand Banks. A watery grave would have been best, and might still be if I can break my oafish husband of his sentimentality.

Fool.

Perhaps one day he will read these journals. Will he be intelligent enough to understand half of what I've written? A third? A quarter?

Yes, perhaps a quarter. But I distract myself with my complaints. I must remain focused on my task. I must not be distracted; it will lead to my ruination.

The oaf must be convinced of the danger the children present. And my father as well. He may balk, and if he does, he shall join them. I've no qualms about manning the lighthouse on my own; I have done so with a new babe in my arms and the oaf drunk with his damnable rum.

Can you imagine it, dear journal? A silent house? A well-kept house without the noise of children or old men? No husband to dirty the sheets. No children to scream for more food. No father to ask for help to the outhouse.

See the lighthouse, her brass gleaming, her bricks white and red so the world will see and know of the danger.

No child suckling at the breast. No husband's rough pawing. No father demanding fealty.

None of it.
None of it.
None of it!

Shane closed the journal. It was nearly noon.

Courtney was stretched out by the tools, her mouth partially open as she slept. Her long lashes kissed the skin beneath her eyes. Her short hair was disheveled.

Beautiful, Shane thought. He put the journal down, took out his cigarettes, and lit one. He tilted his head back a little, exhaled towards the ceiling, and then looked to George.

The younger man sat a little back from the doorway, staring out at the ocean. He had a small cudgel in his hands, the top of it studded with iron nails pounded out of the remains of the lighthouse door. Shane noticed how the man had lost his dazed look, a hard expression on his face.

"George," Shane said softly.

The man looked at him, his eyes dark and haunted.

"How are you holding up?" Shane asked.

George shrugged. "Got nothing to compare it to. Part of me doesn't even believe any of this garbage is real. I mean, come on, ghosts? But then there's the part of me that saw everything, and it's saying, 'Don't be stupid, Stupid.'"

Shane chuckled, nodding. "Yeah. It's a little rough."

"You seem to be doing pretty well with it," George said, looking back out the front door.

"Well, I also grew up in a haunted house," Shane replied.

"Things went bump in the night?" George asked.

"Yeah," Shane said bitterly, "and they eventually killed my parents."

George blushed, and he said, "Sorry, man."

"It's alright," Shane said, upset with himself for mentioning it. *More tired than I thought.*

"So this isn't your first time?" George said.

"No," Shane said. "Not by a long shot. I helped out on a couple of other hauntings, thought I could help with this one, too."

"These ones tougher than you thought?" George asked.

Shane nodded.

"I didn't really think the place was haunted," George said after a short time. "We, me and my friends, we had a website. Murder scenes. Suicides. Stuff like that. People ate it up. Hell, it was how I bought my boat. When we heard about Mike's suicide, we decided we'd come out, get a little video footage. Maybe some pictures of the whole place. We figured we'd do well with this one. The island being isolated and all."

"That's why you showed up yesterday?" Shane asked.

"Yeah," George said, sighing. "Vic and Eric got out of the boat, saw the kid, and started to click away. I told them to get back in the boat. I told them."

George stopped, and Shane waited patiently. Long minutes had passed before George spoke again. When he did, his voice was raw.

"I feel terrible about leaving them," George said, staring out the door. "But they didn't listen to me. And I ran. I had to."

No, Shane thought. *You didn't have to.*

But he kept his opinion to himself.

"I'm worried," George said softly. "Worried I'm going to see them here."

"You might," Shane said.

George's head snapped around, his eyes wide with fear.

"What?" he hissed.

"You might," Shane repeated. "We've already seen the new dead. But I need to see the old dead, and I may be gone for a while."

"What are you talking about?" George asked.

"In the cellar of the keeper's house are five ghosts. The children and father of the ghost, Dorothy."

"Why the hell are they down there?" George said.

"She put their bodies in the cellar after she had murdered them," Shane answered. "They'll be able to tell me more about her. If they have a mind to speak to me."

"You're going down there?" George asked.

"Yes."

"While knowing there are ghosts in it?" George said.

"Yes," Shane said. "I need everything they can give me."

"Information?" George said.

"Yeah," Shane said softly. "And an edge."

"Why do you need an edge?" George said, confused. "I thought we just had to wait until the Coast Guard shows up about the busted light?"

"We will," Shane said. "But I'm going to kill her, too."

George opened his mouth to reply, but he was too surprised for any words to come out.

Chapter 42: Light's Out

Lieutenant Sid Cristo was sitting at the desk outside of the captain's office, playing a losing hand of solitaire. He always played house rules, on the off chance he might actually travel down to one of the casinos in Connecticut, and he rarely won. The captain had been on conference calls all day with command down in Boston, and then with someone else from the Coast Guard Academy in New London.

Sid frowned as he turned over his last hand. He flipped all of the cards over, gathered them into a pile, shuffled, and laid out another game.

As he finished, the door to the office opened.

Sid looked up and was surprised to see an attractive older woman walk in. The dress she wore was short and snug, leaving little to the imagination. She gave him a near-perfect smile, closed the door, and said, "Hello, I've come to tell you there's a technical issue at the Squirrel Island Lighthouse. The contractor I have out there says the wiring may say the light is out."

The solitaire hand was forgotten. "The light's out?"

"No," she said, shaking her head but still smiling. "The wiring may say it is."

"Ma'am," Sid said, "there's no 'maybe.' The light is either on or it's out. The wiring won't send a false signal."

She stepped up closer to the desk, revealing a lot of her ample chest, and winked at him. "Well, even if it is, we don't have to worry about it, do we?"

Sid felt uncomfortably warm, his attention drawn to a locket hanging from around her neck.

"Ma'am," he said, forcing himself to look her in the eyes, "it is something we need to worry about. When the automated system does its check, it'll kick back an alarm here. We need to take care of it as soon as possible."

"Maybe," she said, her voice still seductive, "I should speak with your commanding officer?"

Sid grinned. "Ma'am, I think that would be a wonderful idea."

He pushed himself away from the desk, stood up, and walked to the commander's door. He knocked, opened it, and said, "Captain, we have a person here who wants to speak with you."

Captain Ellen Root glanced up from her desk. "Show them in, please, Lieutenant."

Sid looked back at the civilian, saw the shocked expression on the woman's face, and smiled as politely as possible. "Ma'am, Captain Root will see you now."

He managed not to snicker as she walked dejectedly past him.

Sid sat back down at his desk, looked at the hand he had dealt himself, and started to play.

Chapter 43: A Decision Must Be Made

Amy lay on her bed and stared at the ceiling. She fought the urge to chew on her fingernails, a nervous habit she'd broken herself of twenty years earlier.

Damn it, she thought, sitting up. *What am I going to do? She needs them.*

The desire to see the lighthouse controlled by her family once more burned with the intensity of a fever in Amy's breast. The power of life and death on such a grand scale. There was no greater power in the world, and she and Dorothy would ensure the family had it again. She got up and paced about her bedroom.

When the Coast Guard gets out there, George may still be alive, she told herself. *I don't have to worry about Shane or that girl who's attached herself to him. Just George. George can say I kidnapped him. Threw him there. No one will believe ghosts did any of it. But George can mess it up. He can mess all of it up.*

Amy walked to her closet, flipped on the light, and found an old pair of jeans and sneakers. The sweatshirt she had taken from George's boat lay on the floor. She picked it up, pulled it on, and then dressed quickly. She pulled her hair back in a ponytail, wrapped it around and tucked it up as a bun. A battered Boston Red Sox baseball cap kept her hair up and out of sight.

On her dresser, she found an old pair of black sunglasses and tucked them into the pocket of the sweatshirt. She went over to the bed, knelt down, and pulled her gun safe out. It was a newer model, one equipped with a thumbprint scanner. Amy pressed her right thumb down, heard the satisfying click of the lock letting go, and opened the safe.

She took the small, Glock 9mm out, removed the two fully loaded magazines and a holster, and then locked the safe again. She slid it back under the bed before she stood up. Quietly she loaded the weapon, chambered a round, and made sure the safety was on. The spare magazine went into her back pocket, the pistol into the holster, and the holster into the small of her back clipped to her jeans.

She left the bedroom and grabbed her wallet out of her purse. A quick check showed her license to carry a concealed weapon was in there and up to date. She put the wallet in the front pocket, took the sunglasses out, and put them on.

Amy looked at herself in the mirror by the front door. She didn't have any makeup on. She had washed it all off after her failed attempt at seduction in the Coast Guard's office. Without the makeup, and with her hair put up and away, she was barely recognizable.

They still might recognize you, she cautioned herself, and she nodded in agreement.

True, she replied, *but this task needs to be done.*

She took her keys and left her house. Amy had to get to Squirrel Island as soon as possible. There was a lot of killing she had to do if she was going to correct the situation.

And I have to do it before the Coast Guard gets there, she reminded herself. *Also need to get rid of the bodies. I can't forget that. The souls may remain, but the flesh must go. Yes, it must go, or else no others will be harvested.*

I need to make sure the crops come in, Amy thought, chuckling.

She grinned to herself, broke into a whistle, and made her way to her car.

Chapter 44: Going into the Cellar

"Do you have to go?" Courtney asked softly.

Shane nodded in reply.

"Will you be safe?" she said.

Shane smiled. "I don't know. I hope so. There's no real choice here, though."

"I know." Courtney was standing beside him, her arms folded across her chest as they looked out the doorway at the Atlantic. "You don't need any help?"

"I don't know," Shane said honestly. "I hope I won't, but if you hear screaming, well, I wouldn't mind an assist."

"I'll listen for you. What about him?" she asked, nodding towards George. The man was asleep, propped up between the wall and some of the construction equipment.

"Be careful," Shane said. "They want him more than they want us. I don't know why, but they do. It might just be because they're upset we brought him in here. Don't trust him, though. He'd sell us out in a heartbeat if he thought he could get home safely."

"Will you be careful?" she asked.

"I'll do my best," Shane said. "I've no desire to die here, Cort. Plus we've been having a good time getting to know each other. And I'd like to keep getting to know more about you."

She smirked at him, the tiredness and fear falling away easily, if only briefly. "I like the sound of that, Shane. Make sure you come back here alive and well."

"That's the goal," Shane said. "Alright, wish me luck."

"Luck," Courtney said. Then she reached up, took hold of his face, and pulled him in for a kiss. It was quick but full. No sisterly gesture.

Christ, am I blushing? Shane thought as she let go, his face burning.

"Come back soon," she said.

Shane could only nod, and he stepped out of the relative safety of the lighthouse.

The midmorning air was cool, a strong wind coming in from the east. The waves were still choppy, though not nearly as rough as they had been earlier in the morning.

He glanced around.

Nothing yet, he thought, and he made his way to the keeper's house. He worked around to the back of the building, saw the bulkhead was still open and walked quickly to it. At the top of the narrow stairs, he looked down at the remains of the door. Wood littered the steps and darkness waited for him.

Shane walked down into the cellar and stood in the pale rectangle of light cast by the sun. His own shadow stretched out before him.

"You're back," the grandfather said.

"I am," Shane replied.

"The children aren't here," the unseen ghost said, sadness in his voice. "Their mother came down earlier, in spite of her fear of this place, and frightened them all. They're hiding."

"I'm sorry," Shane said.

"Why have you returned?" the old man asked.

"To ask your name," Shane said, "and to hear what you would tell me about Dorothy."

"My name is Wyatt," the grandfather said. "And what would you like to know about her?"

"Whatever you can tell me," Shane responded, easing himself down into a sitting position on the floor.

"Tell me your name first," Wyatt said, the voice coming closer.

"Shane."

"Well, Shane," Wyatt said, "it is a pleasure. I've had no one but my grandchildren to speak to for a long, long time. I love them, but the conversation of children grows tiresome."

A shape glimmered and Wyatt appeared. He wore a thick, cable-knit sweater, his hair trimmed close to the sides of his head and a little long on the top. On his face, he had impressive muttonchops, the gray hair long and well-cared for. His pants were of some dark material, his shoes worn and black. The hands which extended from the ends of his sweater were large and thick.

"You look as though you are a man of action," Wyatt said as he sat down across from Shane.

"At times," Shane said.

"I appreciate that," Wyatt said, smiling. The expression faded from his face as he looked at Shane.

"I've been dead a long time," Wyatt continued, "though I'm not sure quite for how long exactly."

Shane opened his mouth to tell him the year, but the other man held up a hand and stopped him.

"I don't want to know," Wyatt said. "I'm afraid it would drive me mad, and I'm nearly there already, you see."

Shane hesitated, waited to see if the man would say any more, and when Wyatt didn't, Shane asked, "Will you tell me about your daughter?"

"Let us call her Dorothy, aye, lad?" Wyatt asked softly. "It pains me to think someone I brought into this world would murder her children and family."

"Dorothy it is," Shane said.

"Many thanks," Wyatt said. "What would you know of her?"

"Is she afraid of the cellar because of her husband, or for some other reason?" Shane asked.

"From Clark, not at all," Wyatt said, "her fear is from her mother, I'm afraid."

Shane waited.

"I was a sailor," the man continued. "Away more than I was home, it seemed, and I cannot tell if Dorothy had the devil in her, or if my wife couldn't bother to be a mother. I learned later, much later, of the punishments my wife doled out. She would lock Dorothy in the cellar for days on end. No food. No water. Starved nearly to madness. It was the only way to discipline her, so my wife said. No amount of beatings seemed to silence the girl's tongue. But the cellar, the darkness and hunger. When Dorothy was released, she was cowed. At least for a short time.

"Either way," he continued, "it seems as though Dorothy was

marked. She could feign love. Affection. She could act any role you like. There was nothing in her, though. No spark. She was cold. I've known dogs with more affection than Dorothy Noyes showed the world."

Wyatt cleared his throat, looked past Shane briefly, and smiled tiredly. "It was she who convinced Clark to kill the children. How she did it, I know not. The hard truth is she did, and thus their small bodies are here with me."

Shane looked at the boxes and said in surprise, "Your bodies are still here?"

"Aye," Wyatt said bitterly. "She boxed us up and shipped us out to the mainland. We were kept in darkness, bound in a place where the children screamed and wept. Only recently were we returned to the island, although I cannot say by whom or why."

"My sister Ione," Jillian said, startling Shane as she stepped out of a shadow.

"What?" Wyatt asked, looking at his granddaughter.

The girl, no more than twelve, walked forward and took a seat beside the man. She wore a long nightshirt, the large, heavy curls of her light blonde hair falling to her shoulders. Her face was angular, the cheeks high. Jillian smiled nervously at Shane.

"My sister Ione," she said again. "It was she who had kept our bodies for Mother. Then Ione's grand-daughter returned them."

"How do you know?" Wyatt asked.

"I saw her," Jillian said. "Just once. Ione and her husband were arguing about the boxes, and about how long they would have to keep them in their own cellar."

"What did she say?" Shane asked.

"Until mother called us home," Jillian answered.

Shane looked at Wyatt and said, "When did Dorothy die?"

"I'm not certain," Wyatt replied. "Shortly after she killed Clark, she sent our bodies away."

"You should ask father," Jillian answered. "Mother bound his body with chains and cast him into the ocean, right off the pier."

"Your father's a little upset with me," Shane said. "I broke the lantern."

"He'll speak with you," Jillian said confidentially in a low tone. "He despised mother. I can remember the names he called her when he was dying. They were terrible. Even dead I blushed to hear them."

"Shane," Wyatt said, "why do you want to know?"

Shane got to his feet and smiled at them. "I want her to leave the island."

"She'll never leave," Wyatt said, shaking his head. "It is a fool's errand to try and make her. And how would you? She is much too strong."

"I'll make her," Shane said. "I may need help, but I'll make her go."

"I'll help," Jillian said softly.

"Thank you," Shane said.

"As will I," Wyatt said. "I'm sure the other children will as well. Perhaps even those who have died at Dorothy's hands."

"I would appreciate all of it," Shane said. He glanced at the door and then looked back to Jillian and Wyatt. "She threw him off the pier?"

They both nodded.

"Okay," Shane said, sighing. "I guess I'll go and talk with Clark."

"Come back soon," Jillian said shyly, "I like talking with you."

Shane nodded, smiled, and left the cellar.

Chapter 45: A Time for Action

Amy left her car in the parking garage, cut through an alley between a lobster shop and an antique store, and came out half a block away from the marina. Her disguise was simple and complete. Few people, if any, would recognize her in such plain attire.

I always dress well, she thought, smirking. *They'll never think it was me. And besides, I am on a mission. The family will be returned to the lighthouse. We will be the keepers again, even if we have to wash the island in blood to do it. Who lives. Who dies. What ships make port. All of it will be ours to decide.*

Her smirk faded as she thought of her great-grandmother, the woman hard and brutal, but driven.

She pushes me to greatness, Amy reminded herself. *She won't let me fail.*

A quick peek at the gatehouse showed it was empty, the guard probably on his rounds.

Amy relaxed slightly, set her eyes on George Fallon's Boston Whaler, and moved quickly to it. Her sneakers were almost silent on the worn boards of the dock, the pistol a warm, comforting presence against the small of her back.

When she reached the end of the dock, where the Whaler was tied up, she bent down and went about untying the line.

"Miss?" a voice said from the boat.

Amy stiffened, looked up, and saw the guard who had been on duty early in the morning. He stood on the deck of the boat.

"Yes?" she asked, smiling as she stood up. Out of the corner of her eye, she saw the line snake down and into the water. Her smile broadened.

"Have you seen George around?" he asked. "I came aboard, thinking maybe he was sleeping one off, but he's not here, and he never passed by the gate house. I'm coming up to the close of a twenty-four-hour shift. I haven't seen him at all."

"No," Amy said, "I don't imagine you have. Did you check under the seats?"

"What?" the man said, confused. He twisted to look back and when he did, Amy quickly drew her pistol.

Chapter 46: A Bad Decision

Dell hadn't made too many bad decisions in his life. Joining the Navy had been one of them. Three years of misery and chipping paint. Marrying Mollie Grace, which had been another. Turning his back on the woman who had left George Fallon's Whaler alone in the morning wasn't working out so well either.

Christ on a crutch, Dell thought, staring at the flat, black semi-automatic pistol in her hand. The weapon didn't move, the end of it fixed firmly on his belly.

Dell had seen a man get shot in the gut while on liberty in Hong Kong.

"Miss," Dell said, licking his lips nervously, "I ain't got nothing to steal."

"Step back," she said softly. She didn't wave the gun about. Instead, she made sure it stayed on him.

She'll kill me if I don't do as she says, Dell realized.

Keeping his expression neutral, Dell took a careful step backward and down. He kept his hands at his side, where she could see them.

"Take a seat," she said.

Dell did so.

She climbed aboard easily, her movements graceful. She sat down across from him, the pistol resting on her leg, but still pointing at him.

"What's your name?" she asked, smiling.

"Dell, miss."

"Dell," she said, nodding. "Tell me, can you pilot this boat?"

"Yes, miss," Dell answered.

"Fantastic," she said. She grinned pleasantly at him. "So can I. What you're going to do, Dell, is pilot this little rig out to Squirrel Island."

"Did you kill George there?" he asked suddenly.

"No," she said, laughing. "No. George is alive and well. I promise you that. I also promise you that if you pilot this boat to the island for

138

me, everything will work out for you too."

"And if I don't?" Dell asked nervously.

"Well, Dell," she said politely, "Like I said, I can pilot this boat, too. And, in case you can't figure out what that means, Dell, it means I won't hesitate to put a couple of bullets into your chest and dump you over the side when we're windward to Squirrel Island."

"I'll bring us to the lighthouse," Dell said quickly. "No mistake about that."

"Good," she said, a smile still on her face. "Get up to the helm then and take us out. The sooner we're done, the better we'll all be."

"Yes, miss," Dell said. He stood up on stiff and awkward legs. With a painfully dry throat and his heart thundering against his ribs, Dell went to the helm.

Bring her out there, Dell, he told himself, *bring her out there and be done with her.*

Aye, he thought, *best plan there is.*

Dell started the engine and backed the boat slowly out of her berth.

Chapter 47: A Discussion

Shane walked around the front of the keeper's house, wary for any of the dead who might be wandering. All he saw was Courtney in the doorway of the lighthouse. She lifted a hand in greeting, and he waved and smiled at her.

Her smile was tight and forced.

She worries, Shane thought, turning his attention to the pier. The young woman's concern made him feel cared for, a curious sensation. Even when he had briefly dated Marie Lafontaine it had been more physical than anything else.

Focus, Shane scolded himself. He followed the path down to the pier, walked to the end of it and sat down. His legs hung over the side, and a fine mist was picked up by the wind and cast on him with each wave as it broke. Clumsily he took out his cigarettes, lit one, and enjoyed the potent chemicals in the smoke.

"Clark Noyes," Shane said, speaking towards the ocean, "can you hear me?"

"Aye, you git," came Clark's voice from behind him, "I can hear you."

Shane twisted slightly, saw Clark standing a few feet back and asked politely, "Will you sit with me, Clark?"

"Tell me why you have a mind to speak with me now," Clark said warily. "You ruined my light."

"I ruined your light," Shane replied, "because Dorothy wants the rest of us dead. And, no offense now, but I have no desire to be dead yet."

Clark nodded. "Aye, understandable."

"As for why I want to speak with you," Shane continued, "I want to know how you died."

Clark raised an eyebrow over one charred eye, then he grinned, the cracked lips twisting obscenely. "I like you, Shane, I do. And if my foul bride wants you dead, well, perhaps we can upset her a bit in that

140

regard."

Clark walked forward and took a seat beside Shane.

The cold emanating from the ghost was highly unpleasant but bearable.

"I have to tell you," Clark said after a minute of silence, "I loved being a keeper. I enjoyed the solitude. I am not a good man, Shane. Nor am I a pleasant one. Are you looking to see remorse in me?"

"No," Shane answered truthfully. "I've known a lot of bad men, Clark. Not many as bad as you, mind you, but bad enough. And one or two worse. God judges. Not me."

"Just and true, and true and just," Clark said, nodding. "Now, you want to know how I died?"

"I do."

"My wife," Clark said, looking out over the Atlantic. "My blushing bride. My own Eve, the lover of the serpent. She killed me. Tortured me first, though I deserved it."

"How did she torture you?" Shane asked, already knowing the answer.

"The light," Clark said bitterly. "My own light. Burned the sight out of my eyes. Starved me. Bled me. Gelded me. Thus my body is now the horror you behold."

"Why are you still here?" Shane asked.

"She bound me," Clark said, his voice thick with anger. "A soul to keep the lighthouse working true. Nothing more than a slave."

"And what of her?" Shane asked. "Did she work the light after your death?"

"Not for long," Clark spat. "The coastal watch, they found her out. And she killed herself, damn her! She bound herself to the island, made sure she would be here."

"And you never were able to care for the lighthouse again?" Shane asked.

Clark shook his head. "Even with the binding of the man, Dane, she hasn't let me back in! And then you went and broke the thrice-damned light."

"I did," Shane agreed, keeping an eye on the ghost. "I did. But I've already told you, in order to be rescued. They'll be coming today, tonight the latest, to repair the lantern. And if you help me, Clark, I'll be able to shatter Dorothy the way I did the light."

Clark looked at him warily. "How?"

"You feel that anger inside of you? That hate?" Shane asked.

Clark nodded.

"I'll need some of it, the part you hold against her," Shane said softly. "The part all of you hold against her."

"And what will happen?" Clark said. "When you have this?"

"I'll break her," Shane replied grimly. "I will pull her apart and drive each piece like a nail into Hell."

Clark stared at Shane for several long minutes. Shane tightened his grip on the knuckledusters, readied his make-shift weapon, and waited.

"Can you do it?" Clark asked finally.

"I can," Shane answered.

"Have you done it before?" The skepticism in Clark's voice was thick.

"Once," Shane said, "and that little girl was a hell of a lot worse than Dorothy could ever think to be."

Clark raised an eyebrow, then a cold, hard smile crept onto his face. "The lighthouse will be mine?"

"The lighthouse and the whole damned island for all I care," Shane said truthfully. "I'll not chase you from it. I only want Dorothy, she's the one pulling the strings here."

"Aye," Clark said softly, "that she is. A mad witch playing at Fate."

In a louder voice, Clark said, "You'll have my help, Shane. For my lighthouse, and more than a bit of revenge."

"Fair enough," Shane said. He stood up. "If you'll excuse me, I have others to speak to about Dorothy."

"There are those you don't know," Clark said, standing. "They won't heed your call, nor believe you."

"Will you help?"

"To put my bride in Hell?" Clark asked, then with a wicked grin he said, "Of course I will."

The ghost vanished, and Shane was alone on the pier. He looked out at the Atlantic, saw the sun moving steadily towards the western horizon and thought, *Will they come tonight for the light? Will it even matter in the end?*

He shrugged, unable to answer his own questions, and turned to walk back to the lighthouse.

Chapter 48: An Uneasy Alliance

Courtney stood in the doorway of the lighthouse, watching Shane. The man was walking slowly along the pier, his head bent down. She had seen him speak to the ghost, and while she knew Shane would tell her what was said, she still burned with curiosity.

A grumble behind her caused her to take her attention away from Shane and to George Fallon.

The man was sitting up, yawning and rubbing at his eyes. When he lowered his hands, he nodded to her and looked dejectedly at the doorway.

"What's going on out there?" George asked tiredly.

"Shane's on his way back," she answered.

George nodded. He sighed and said, "I wish I'd never come out here."

Courtney didn't reply.

"How'd you get on the island?" he asked.

"Bad decisions," she answered. "Ones that seemed like they were good ideas at the time."

"Same here," George said.

"Hello," Shane said, stepping into the doorway and resting a hand on the small of Courtney's back.

The touch was gentle, but firm, and sent a thrill of excitement through her.

"What's going on?" she asked, her voice steady.

Shane quickly explained how Clark had agreed to help.

"I'll need to try and find some of the others," he continued. "Dane and Eileen, even Scott, if he'll listen to me."

"Will it work?" George asked, his tone one of disbelief.

Shane nodded. "What are the names of your friends?"

"Vic and Eric," George said. "But how is it going to work?"

"You're in construction, right?" Shane asked.

George nodded.

"So you know what a power converter is, AC to DC when you need the electricity in a pinch?" Shane said.

"Sure," George said. "What's that got to do with this place?"

"I think that I'm some kind of a power converter," Shane said. "Before, when I had enough information, when I had the backing of other ghosts, I was able to channel it. And that power, well it forces the dead, like Dorothy, into a somewhat physical form I can handle."

George shook his head. "That doesn't make any sense at all."

"Do ghosts?" Courtney asked. "I mean, seriously, do ghosts make any sense to you whatsoever? They shouldn't even be here, let alone be capable of hurting someone. But they are, and they do."

George didn't respond.

"Whether it makes sense or not," Shane said. "It's what happened."

"And you've done it before?" George said doubtfully.

"Once," Shane replied.

"You managed to get rid of the ghost?" George said.

"If I hadn't," Shane said coldly, "I wouldn't be here."

"How can you do something like that?" Courtney asked. She looked at the man before her as he hesitated before answering her.

"I think it has something to do with my house," Shane said slowly, seeming to pick each word with care. "I never had a great knack for languages before we moved to Berkley Street. I could speak English, of course, but nothing else. Then, the more time I spent at the house, and the older I got, the more I understood. The more I could speak the different languages. It felt like something was unlocked in my head."

"I've done research on what I did at my house," Shane continued. "There are skills, like mine, which have been recorded. Others who can channel energy. There are a few accounts online. Usually they pass along a family line. My parents didn't say anything about it, and my grandparents on both sides were dead."

"So maybe this is genetic?" Courtney asked.

"That's what it looks like," Shane said, nodding. "The stories I read talked about how most benevolent ghosts don't have a problem with people who possess my ability. It's the bad ones, like Dorothy, who really don't care for us. I don't think she's realized what I can do. I don't think she would leave me be."

"So what are you going to do?" George asked, skepticism still in his voice.

"I'm going to learn more about Dorothy," Shane said, looking at Courtney, "if I can really know her, then I'm almost positive I can do it again. Make her, well, touchable."

Courtney moved closer to Shane, tilting her head slightly to look at him. "You're going to go speak with more?"

Shane nodded.

"Do you need help?" she asked.

Shane smiled at her, teeth stained by coffee, but the smile was genuine.

"No, thank you," he said gently. "I'd rather you were here. They seem to avoid the lighthouse, although I'm not quite sure why."

"Okay," Courtney said. She looked over at George. The man was looking listlessly at the floor. To Shane, she said, "You'll be careful?"

"As careful as I can be," Shane said. He leaned in and gave her a soft kiss. "I'll be back."

Courtney nodded, her back cold after he took his hand away and left the lighthouse. She glanced at George, saw the man was still concerned with the floor, and sat down inside the doorway. The ocean stretched out beyond the island, but in the distance, she saw a boat.

It was heading toward the island.

Chapter 49: Terminal Fleet

"There's a boat," Courtney said.

George looked up past the girl, out the doorway and onto the Atlantic.

She's right, George realized. A boat was steadily making its way to the island. The closer the boat came, the more familiar it looked.

"Oh my God," George whispered.

"What?" Courtney asked.

"That's my boat," George said, recognizing the antennae array and the Gadsden flag snapping proudly off the aft of *Terminal Fleet*. "That's *my* boat!"

He got to his feet, his heart beating excitedly.

"George," Courtney said, standing up. "Didn't she steal the boat? The woman who dumped you here?"

A chill raced through him as he realized the girl was right. He was nodding when the boat got close enough for him to see the one piloting it.

"But that's not her," George said excitedly. "That's Dell! That's Dell! He's the gatekeeper at the marina!"

George raced out of the lighthouse, pushing past Courtney. He stumbled, nearly fell, but caught himself. He hurried down the path to the pier, his feet hitting the wood at the same time as Dell pulled the Boston Whaler in alongside.

"Dell!" George shouted.

Dell raised his hand in greeting, a smile of relief on his face.

Then a shot was fired, and George watched as the top half of Dell's face exploded outwards. Blood, bone, and brain sprayed outward.

Someone was screaming, and George realized he was the one making the noise.

The smile never left the ruins of Dell's face, even as he collapsed to the deck. From one of the seats, the woman who had marooned George on Squirrel Island stood up. In her hand was a small, black, semi-automatic pistol. She shook ever so slightly as the boat ran aground slightly and came to a sharp stop.

A broad, happy smile was plastered on her face, and she waved cheerfully to him.

"Hello, George!" she said, stepping onto the pier and keeping the pistol on him. She quickly made the boat fast, stretched, and said, "You have an appointment to keep with my great-grandmother. She's not one you want to anger, I might add. No, she's worse than Bruce Banner when she's angry."

She raised the pistol a little, so George was staring at it rather than her.

"No," the woman said, "let's find her, shall we? We don't want you being any later than you already are. She wants one of her newly dead to kill you, George. The dear woman enjoys watching their initiations. Tremendously."

George went to speak, but only a moan came out. A warm liquid rushed down his pants and he realized he had wet himself.

Chapter 50: Interrupted

Shane had only left Courtney a few minutes earlier when he heard the gunshot, followed by a brief, horrified scream.

All plans to meet with the dead were cast aside as he turned and ran back towards the pier. When he reached the edge of the lighthouse he paused, crept around the building, and looked down at the pier.

A boat, whose engine he had never heard, was tied up to the pier. George was there, his shoulders slumped as Amy pointed a handgun at him. A quick glance at the boat showed a body near the helm.

Shane pulled his knuckledusters off, stuffed them into his back pocket, looked around, and saw a fist-sized rock on the ground. He picked it up, found the weight to be good, and took a long look at Amy.

She and George were talking, but the wind carried their words away.

When she brought the pistol up a little higher, Shane stepped out and threw the stone. It raced through the air, a perfect, elongated arc.

With a flat crack, it smashed into the side of Amy's head. Her legs collapsed beneath her, and she fell with a thud to the pier. Her hand let go of the pistol, and the weapon slid off the wood and into the ocean.

George sat down, his shoulders shaking.

Christ, Shane thought as he walked back to the path, *he's absolutely worthless.*

Courtney came out of the lighthouse and joined Shane.

"Did you just hit her with a rock?" she asked.

"Yup," Shane said.

"That was an awesome throw!"

Shane grinned. "Thanks. I was trying to hit her in the chest, though."

"Whatever works," Courtney said. "We've got a boat now."

"Oh damn," Shane said, surprised. "We do!"

The two of them walked quickly down onto the pier. George was staring at the boat.

"What's wrong?" Shane asked, dropping to a knee and checking Amy's pulse. She had a welt on the side of her head, and blood trickled from her nose.

"She killed Dell," George said, his voice low and hoarse.

"She didn't kill you," Shane said harshly, "and she didn't kill us. That your boat?"

George nodded.

"Well let's get the hell out of here," Shane said. He picked up Amy and draped her over his shoulder.

"Okay," George agreed. Courtney helped him to his feet.

"You won't be using this little boat," a voice said from the Boston Whaler.

Shane looked for the owner, and he saw the young boy with the pipe who had killed George's friends. The boy stood on the deck, pipe in his mouth as he grinned.

"And why won't we?" Shane asked.

"She's sinking, she is," the boy said. "When your bonnie lass there shot the pilot, well, the boat ran aground. She sprang a good and healthy leak, and not one to be fixed without a dry dock."

Shane looked at the boat and saw the boy was right.

It is sinking, Shane thought. As he watched, it had sank perhaps half an inch, and then half an inch more. In silence, they all stood where they were and after several minutes the boat had settled down as far as she would go.

"That's a little bit of a disappointment, is it not?" the boy asked gleefully.

Shane wanted to strangle him.

"It is," Shane agreed, his voice tight. "But that's alright. It's better to finish the job myself than leave it to another."

The boy took the pipe out of his mouth, laughed pleasantly, and pointed the stem at Shane. "That, my fine bucko, is an excellent way to look at this particular situation. You've no love for Dorothy?"

Shane shook his head.

"Aye," the boy said, and then he winked. "Neither do I. She's a right foul beast, she is. I heard your little talk with Clark Noyes. You mean to do her in."

"I do," Shane said.

"Good," the boy said, returning his pipe to his mouth. "Good. I'll see you at the end, then."

The boy vanished.

"I am more than a little upset," Courtney said.

Shane nodded. "Same here."

George began to cry.

Chapter 51: George Makes a Move

George spat on the ground outside of the lighthouse, his back against the brick wall. Behind him, inside the building, Shane and Courtney sat with the woman, Amy. The one who had tried to kill him.

Not once, George thought miserably, *but twice. How would Shane like it?* George thought. *If someone was trying to kill him?*

He felt ashamed at having cried in front of them, but at least Amy hadn't seen it.

The sun was sinking rapidly on the horizon, the waves of the Atlantic reflecting the day's last light. The chrome and steel of his boat shining as well.

George straightened up as he looked at *Terminal Fleet.*

The antennae which still stood tall in the evening light.

The radios! he thought excitedly. George glanced back into the lighthouse. Shane and Courtney sat close together. Against the back wall, her hands bound behind her back, Amy was still unconscious.

I'll check the radios, George decided. *Maybe then Baldy won't sneer at me.*

George nodded to himself and quickly walked away from the building. He hurried down the path, moved as quietly as he could across the pier, and reached his Boston Whaler. He paused and looked at it, wincing at the sight of it.

Christ, he thought, sighing, *I'll have to have a salvage crew come out, lift her, and tow her back in.*

He scrambled aboard and came to a sharp stop.

Dell's body was on the deck. Mercifully, the man was face down, but the remnants of his skull and brain were splattered over the helm. Hundreds of flies crawled about the exposed flesh while what looked like thousands had already begun to feast and lay eggs on Dell. The entire boat stank of death. George turned and vomited onto the pier, clutching the side of the Whaler.

With bile dripping down his chin and clinging to the corners of his mouth, George turned back to the wreckage of Dell and the radios.

"Oh Christ, Dell," George whispered, "I'm so sorry this happened to you."

Gingerly, he stepped over the body and threw up on the deck as he tried to wipe dried brains off of the two-way radio.

"It won't work," a woman said from behind him.

George twisted around, his sneakers slipping in the blood and bile, and he sat down on Dell's head. Bone cracked loudly, and the flies took to the air, buzzing around him angrily.

Fresh tears sprang into George's eyes, and he scrambled away, his pants wet with blood and urine.

A young woman stood near the port side. She was pretty, but her eyes were closed, and it looked as though she had been crying as well.

Something's wrong, George thought, squinting.

Oh, he realized, *I can see through her.*

Right through her.

She took a step forward and he crab-walked backward until he bumped into the starboard side.

Her eyes looked deflated, and her neck was bent oddly to one side.

"There's no service here," the young woman said. "None. It's why we couldn't get any help. There's no way to get in touch with anyone."

"What happened to you?" George whispered.

"Me?" she asked, smiling. "Oh, Dorothy happened to me. She put out my eyes and broke my neck."

"Why?" George asked, his voice barely audible.

"Why not?" the young woman asked, shrugging. She stopped a foot away from him and said confidently, "I will tell you this, though."

"What?"

"This is how it felt," she whispered, and before George could move she grabbed hold of his head.

Frozen thumbs worked their way up to his eyes and pushed.

George screamed.

Chapter 52: Then There Were Two

A loud, horrified scream jerked Shane's attention away from the unconscious Amy. As he and Courtney looked to the door, he said angrily, "Damn it!"

Courtney didn't ask why.

Both of them could see George was gone.

Shane kept a tight grip on his temper, and he stood up and went to the door. He glanced around and saw movement on the defunct boat.

Eileen stood over George, her hands on his head.

"What's she doing?" Courtney asked, fear thick in her voice.

"Killing him," Shane said. He put his hands gently on Courtney and turned her away. George's screams ended abruptly. Shane shook his head.

"It's too late," Shane said softly. He and Courtney sat down slowly.

For several long minutes, they were silent.

And then Amy let out a grunt, rolled from her side onto her back, and opened her eyes. She blinked several times, the camping light close to her and shining brightly.

"Hello, Sunshine," Shane said softly.

Amy's eyes focused on him, and her face paled. She went to move her arms and couldn't. Shane watched the color drain from her lips as she pressed them tightly together. The dark, dried blood on the side of her face stood out boldly.

Amy looked at him, wet her lips and said, "Hi Shane."

"Courtney," Shane said, "this is Amy. Amy, this is Courtney."

"A pleasure," Amy said, forcing a smile. "I don't suppose you'd do a girl a favor and untie me?"

"No," Shane said. "You're all trussed up, and I'd like to keep it that way."

"Why?" she asked, feigning ignorance. "Why would you keep me tied up?"

"Who do you think hit you with a rock?" Courtney snapped.

"You did?" Amy asked, glaring at Courtney.

"I did," Shane said, correcting her. "I have more than half a mind to drown you, Amy, but I don't want to add another body to this damned place."

"That would be murder," Amy said. She focused her attention on him.

"And so it would," Shane agreed. "I'd sleep alright. You, Courtney?"

Courtney nodded.

"So, you know where we stand on the whole murder issue, Amy," Shane said. "I know where you stand on it, too."

"Shane," she said, her voice low and seductive. "You don't think I could have had anything to do with murder, do you?"

"Amy," Shane said, leaning closer. "I have something I want to tell you."

"What?" she asked, smiling at him.

"I guarantee you I will beat the brains right out of your head," Shane said coldly, "if I think, even for an instant, that Courtney is going to die here."

Amy sat back sharply. "She's going to kill all of us."

"Dorothy?" Shane asked.

Amy nodded.

"I think you're mistaken," Shane said sincerely.

Amy looked at him, confusion on her face.

"I already told you," Shane said, "I'll kill you. Not Dorothy."

"You don't understand!" Amy shouted.

The sudden violence in her voice caused Shane to recoil briefly.

"What don't we understand?" Courtney asked, her knuckles whitening as she tightened her grip on her cudgel.

"My family," Amy said, a mad gleam creeping into her eyes. "This island is ours. This lighthouse, it is ours. All of it. Even the dead. It is our purpose, our divine mission, to ensure the light forever shines. By controlling the light, we decide who lives, who dies upon the seas, and who will drown within the depths."

"Each death grants Dorothy strength. With each soul trapped on the island, her power grows. And the more dead upon the island," Amy continued, grinning, "the stronger my great-grandmother becomes. Soon, she shall be able to leave the island, to travel freely to the land, where her power will grow ten-fold. Thus, we ensure the safety of the light."

"And what about me breaking it?" Shane asked, taking out a cigarette.

Amy sneered. "A mere speed bump in our goal. The Coast Guard will come out. They will fix it. We will guard it. Dorothy will see to it."

Shane blew streams of smoke out of his nose, grinned at her, and said, "Are you planning on being alive for this whole deal, or are you expendable, too?"

"She won't sacrifice me," Amy spat. "I brought the lighthouse back into our family. I returned her children to her."

"Her children?" Courtney asked, looking at Shane. "Dorothy had children?"

Shane nodded.

Courtney switched her attention to Amy. "Why does she need her children?"

Amy smiled and remained quiet.

"Now, you decide to shut up?" Shane asked. "No. I don't like that."

"And what will you do about it, Shane?" Amy asked softly, laughing. "Will you torture it out of me?"

"Yup," Shane said, nodding. "I hate how sweaty I get, but I'll deal with it."

Amy's eyes widened. "You're joking."

He shook his head. "Not in the least little bit. Courtney?"

"Yes?" Courtney asked.

"I'm going to ask you to turn around and watch the doorway for me. I'll gag the murderer here, but you're still going to hear some things," Shane said apologetically.

Courtney looked hard at him, hesitated, and then nodded. "Alright."

She turned around and faced the doorway.

Shane took his cigarette out of his mouth, slipped his shirt off, and smiled at Amy. He returned his cigarette to its proper place, twisted the shirt into a tight length and got to his feet.

Amy pushed herself backward as far as she could go.

"Stay away from me!" she snarled, jerking her head from side to side as he got closer. She kicked at him, but the blows were weak, bouncing impotently off of his shins and knees.

He extended his arms, and as the shirt neared her mouth Amy screamed, "Wait!"

Shane stopped. The shirt was only a few inches from her head.

Panting, Amy glared at him.

"Is there something you want to tell me?" Shane asked softly.

She nodded.

"Well?" he said.

Amy closed her eyes and whispered, "She needs to have the children placed at the cardinal points."

"Of the compass?" Shane asked.

"Yes."

"Why?" Shane said.

"It locks the power in," Amy replied. "All of the strength Dorothy's gathered over the years. All of the deaths. The fear and horror. It feeds her. With it, she'll be able to power the lighthouse's lantern even if there's no power in the solar batteries. Even if the backup generator has been run dry. She'll be able to keep the light shining.

"She'll be able to save the ships," Amy whispered, finally opening her eyes again.

"Well," Shane said, unraveling his shirt. "She's more civic-minded than I thought."

"God told her what to do," Amy said, the fervent gleam returning to her eyes. "It is our mission, Shane. You can't stop it. You mustn't."

He shrugged, finished his cigarette, and stubbed it out on the stairwell. Sighing, he slipped the shirt back on and said, "Courtney."

"What's up?" the young woman asked, stepping away from the doorway.

"We need to go down to George's boat, together," Shane said. "There should be some emergency supplies, a flare gun, and all that good stuff."

"Okay," Courtney said. She switched the cudgel from one hand to the other.

"Why do you need the flare gun?" Amy asked.

"So we can signal the Coast Guard," Shane said. "If they're not on their way already, the flare gun will definitely light a fire under them."

"You can't," Amy said, horrified. "She's not ready yet."

"Perfect timing then," Shane said with a grin.

"You can't!" Amy shrieked.

Shane winked at her, turned away, and said to Courtney, "Ready?"

Courtney nodded, and together they left the lighthouse. Behind them, Amy screamed furiously.

Chapter 53: Waiting for Dorothy

Amy dropped her chin to her chest and sobbed. She was enraged.

They'll try and ruin it all, she thought. *They'll destroy every last bit of it. Everything!*

The temperature in the lighthouse dropped and the locket around her neck grew cold, her breastbone aching painfully from the touch of the metal.

Amy whimpered and forced herself to look up.

Dorothy stood in front of her. Beside her was the shattered remains of a man. Amy kept her eyes focused on her great-grandmother.

"Amy," Dorothy said.

"Yes?" Amy's voice was barely above a whisper.

"You came back to finish off George?" Dorothy asked.

"Yes."

"But you did not," Dorothy said.

Amy couldn't respond. She shivered with fear.

"One of the new children did," Dorothy said after a moment. "The one named Eileen. She took care of George for us."

Amy looked up at her great-grandmother, unable to contain her surprise. "She did?"

Dorothy nodded.

"What about Shane?" Amy asked fearfully. "What about the girl, Courtney?"

"What of them?" Dorothy asked. "We've only to slay them both. He will look like a murderer, and then another suicide. It is a task which is easy enough to manage."

"And what about me?" Amy asked. "Will you untie me?"

Dorothy shook her head. "You must stay bound. Perhaps for a day, perhaps less. You need to be found as you are. Only then will you be able to play the role of victim. The deaths of the man named George, his colleagues, and those from the yacht. All of them can then be laid at the feet of Shane. It is he who will be the suicide victim this time."

Amy nodded. "So I wait."

"So you wait," Dorothy agreed. "Now this one and I must carry out the rest of the task. Be at ease, child; you have done our family proud."

Amy blushed with pride. Dorothy and the mutilated man vanished. The locket on around her neck grew warm. Soon the chill of the room was replaced by the warm June air.

Smiling, Amy closed her eyes and did her best to ignore the discomfort of her arms and wrists.

Chapter 54: A Missing Light

Chief Petty Officer Al Arsenault looked out at Squirrel Island.

The lighthouse was dark. The signal from the island's service program was correct. Something was wrong with the lantern.

He turned away from the window, picked up the phone and called Captain Root at home. Al quickly informed her of the situation, and the Captain responded in the same fashion. In less than two minutes, the phone call was over, and Al turned to Seaman Mauser.

"Mauser," Al said.

The young man looked up from a battered paperback. "Chief?"

"Call down to Zucci, let him know we need the patrol boat readied," Al said, sitting down at his desk.

"Aye, Chief," Mauser said.

Al took a drink of his coffee. Mauser made the call, then he looked over at Al and said, "Zucci wants to know who we need?"

Al put his mug down and said, "We'll need at least a two-person tech crew. Light's out on Squirrel Island. May be just a couple of wires, or it may be the lantern itself."

Mauser nodded and relayed the information, then hung up the phone. "Anything else, Chief?"

"Yeah," Al said, finishing his drink. "Put another pot on, will you, Mauser? Looks like it's going to be a long night."

"You got it, Chief." The young man got up and left the office. Al went to the window again and looked out at Squirrel Island. He'd been there a few times, and each occasion was something he'd rather forget.

The place was cold.

Bad luck, Al thought. *A Jonah's place if ever there was one. Nothing but death there. The quicker this is done, the better.*

Mauser returned a short time later. "Coffee should be ready in about five, Chief."

Al nodded his thanks, but he didn't move away from the window. The lighthouse was a dark silhouette against the stars. The sea had calmed down, the waves no longer rough.

Al yawned, and the phone rang. Mauser answered it and said, "Zucci says the boat's ready whenever you are. The crew is already aboard."

"Good," Al said, turning away from the window. "Tell Zucci I'll be down there in five minutes."

Mauser nodded and relayed the message.

Al took his travel mug off of his desk and brought it into the staff room.

Well, he thought, *let's get this done with.*

Chapter 55: Strange News

Marie Lafontaine sat in her chair, a glass of wine in her hand as she watched the ten o'clock news. She was only half listening, more focused on whether or not she could finish her drink before she had to go to bed. The day had been long and frustrating. A witness had recanted their statement, and another person had overdosed on heroin.

In the tot-lot playground on Ash Street, Marie thought, shaking her head.

The words 'mysterious disappearance' were spoken by the newscaster and caught Marie's attention. She listened as the reporter talked about how a gatekeeper at a marina in Maine had disappeared from work.

The news station used a stock photo of the marina. Beyond the docked boats and wooden pier, Marie caught sight of something which sent a bitter fear through her. The Squirrel Island lighthouse formed part of the backdrop.

Marie picked up her cellphone and called Amy. It went right to voicemail. She ended the call, got up, and walked over to her laptop. Marie did a quick search for more information on the disappearance, but she received nothing more than the man's name and basic history.

She frowned and then searched for information on the empty yacht which was found. The articles she found all agreed on one particular point.

No bodies had been found. No lifeboat. No distress signal sent out. The crew was still missing.

Did Amy get this guy to bring her out to the island to check on Shane? Marie wondered. *But wouldn't he have told someone?*

Something's wrong, Marie realized. *Terribly wrong.*

She knocked back the last of her wine, put the empty glass on the desk beside the laptop, and made her way to the bedroom.

It was time to drive to Maine.

Chapter 56: Slipping Away

Although Courtney felt better to be with Shane, she wasn't naïve enough to believe all of her troubles would be solved by being with him.

Mom always told you to rely on yourself, Courtney thought. *Don't expect a prince to come and rescue you.*

Courtney looked at Shane and grinned.

No, she thought, *he's no prince. More like a hired gunman than anything else.*

And Courtney liked that about him.

As they made their way towards the pier, she forced herself to pay attention. George's boat was still visible, still partially submerged.

And still completely useless, she thought, sighing.

They reached the pier and Shane led them swiftly to the boat. At its side, he paused, turned, and said, "Stop here, Courtney."

"Why?" she asked, halting a few feet from him.

"Because it's bad," he said. "Terribly so."

"I can help," Courtney said, the words coming out quickly.

"You do help, and you will," Shane said, not looking away from her. "I just don't think you need to see any more bodies."

"More bodies?" Courtney asked. "I thought it was only George."

"And the man who brought Amy here this morning," Shane said.

"What about him?" Courtney said.

"She blew his brains out," Shane said. "Bullet to the back of the skull. Exit through the front. His brains and skull are everywhere."

"Oh," Courtney said. She glanced at the boat, but she didn't try to look in it. "You'll be able to find what you need without me going on board?"

"Yes," Shane said. "Stay here, and stay safe."

She nodded. Shane stepped forward, embraced her, and then stepped away. She watched as he climbed up onto the deck. Soon he was gone, and she could hear him rummaging through the interior of the boat. Long minutes passed, and she shifted her attention constantly from the boat to the pier, from the pier to the lighthouse, from the lighthouse to the cabin, and then back again.

"Got it!" Shane called up.

Courtney heard his feet on the ladder and in a second, he was back on the deck. He had an emergency kit in his hands. She took it from him, and he climbed down to stand on the dock. They sat down, opened the kit, and looked at the materials inside. Among the emergency supplies, they found a small strobe light, emergency rations, a flare gun, and a compressed emergency raft with instructions on how to inflate it. It even had a collapsible paddle.

"Perfect," Shane said softly.

"How so?" Courtney asked.

"The raft," Shane said, looking at her. "We're going to inflate it, get you a life vest from the boat, and send you out a little off shore."

"What?" Courtney said in disbelief. "You can't be serious?"

"I am," Shane said. "If you're in the raft, you can't be grabbed by the dead. They won't even care. You'll be able to use the flare gun, and someone will come and pick you up."

"What about you?" Courtney asked. "You can't stay here by yourself."

"I have to," Shane said. "I have to take care of Dorothy, and you need to tell whoever picks you up that it's Amy's fault. All of it."

"Do I try to tell them about the ghosts?" Courtney asked, and winced at how ridiculous it sounded even to her.

"No," Shane said, shaking his head. "Don't tell them about the ghosts. Tell them how you became trapped here, and how she kept you a prisoner."

"Not much of a stretch there," Courtney said bitterly.

"No," Shane agreed, "not much at all."

"And if they ask me if she killed my friends," Courtney said, "I'll tell them yes."

Shane nodded.

"Are you going to be safe?" Courtney asked him, worry spiking through her as she looked at him.

His face was harsh, the light of the stars and the moon etching shadows on his pale skin. "Probably not," Shane said. "But we'll make it work."

She wanted to say more, but she didn't.

"Alright," Shane said softly, "let's get this started."

He picked up the raft, pulled the cord, and a sharp hiss sounded as the rubber inflated rapidly. With an easy motion, he dropped it onto the opposite side of the pier, holding onto a long, nylon tether.

Silently Courtney picked up the emergency rations and the flare gun.

"Here," Shane said, passing the tether to her. "Hold this for a second."

When she took it, Shane scrambled back onto George's boat and came back quickly with a life vest. He helped her put it on, tightened the straps across her chest, and smiled at her.

"As soon as you're in the raft, I'll pass the paddle to you. I want you to make your way about a hundred yards out. More if you can. Once you're there, fire off the flare gun, and move out a little more, okay?" he asked.

Courtney nodded.

"Good," Shane said, smiling. He took her face in his hands, looked into her eyes, and said, "Be safe. Don't worry about me."

She went to nod, but he held her still, bent forward, and kissed her full and long on the lips.

"No fear, Courtney," he whispered. "Fear kills."

Shane let go, and Courtney went to get into the raft, heart beating fiercely.

Chapter 57: Amongst the Enemy

Only when Shane turned to walk back up the pier did he realize Courtney had left her cudgel.

Too late, he thought grimly, picking the weapon up. He looked back at her in the bright orange circular raft. The strobe light, attached to the top by a cord, pulsed brightly in the night sky. *Too dangerous to call her back.*

He shook his head at his own forgetfulness and pushed aside thoughts of her being dead because of it. With the cudgel on his shoulder, he reached the end of the pier and paused.

I need to go back into the cellar again, Shane thought. *I need to tell the children what their mother's plan is.*

He turned to walk up and around the side of the house and saw them.

Four men.

One was George Fallon, whose eyes were gone. The others were the man's friends. Both of them looked as well as could be expected, but Shane knew they had been drowned. The fourth was the man who brought Amy back to the island, and the majority of his forehead and orbital sockets were missing.

"And where are you going?" George asked, blindly staring at him.

"Wherever I want," Shane replied pleasantly. "And yourselves?"

"She wants you dead," George answered. "It's not fair that you're alive, and we're dead."

"You know," Shane said, moving the cudgel off of his shoulder, "I have to say, life, in general, isn't fair. So, I'm not particularly surprised that death isn't fair either."

"You're going to kill yourself," one of the other men said, "whether you want to or not."

"Interesting statement," Shane said. "Do you have any intention of backing that up?"

The man who had spoken grinned maliciously and walked forward.

Are they stupid enough to attack one at a time? Shane wondered. When the other three remained where they were, Shane grinned and said, "Thank you."

The approaching man paused, confused. "Why?"

Shane swung the cudgel, full force at him, and the ghost screamed as it tore through.

As their friend vanished, the other three men attacked.

It came fast and hard, and though they lacked the brutality and effectiveness of the Mujahedeen he had faced in Afghanistan, the men were no less determined.

A searing pain ripped through his left arm, and it felt as though someone was trying to tear the muscle off of his bone. Another blow struck his leg and dropped him to a knee while a third blow struck his shoulder, his fingers springing open, the cudgel falling to the ground.

Grimacing, Shane swung his numb right hand, the iron knuckledusters causing the faceless man to vanish. An explosion of pain erupted behind his eyes, and Shane screamed angrily, lashing out with his left hand. The gauntlet made from the hinge shattered George, leaving Shane with the last ghost.

Shane spat on the ground and looked at the man, who glared at Shane.

"How did you do that?" the man hissed.

"Do what?" Shane asked. "Send your little buddies away?"

The man nodded, looking around as if he was expecting help.

"Iron," Shane said, grinning, the pain in his head receding. "It does a body good."

Before the man could respond, Shane threw himself forward, the knuckleduster passing through the man.

Shane was left alone on the path, his body aching.

Cellar, he told himself. *Get to the cellar, and then deal with Dorothy.*

Chapter 58: Shock and Horror

Amy was half in and out of sleep when a cold, hard slap woke her up.

Her eyes snapped open, and she found Dorothy above her. The woman's face was a mask of rage.

"Who is he?" her great-grandmother roared.

Amy scrambled backward. "Who?"

"Shane, Shane Ryan!" Dorothy hissed, slapping Amy again.

Amy winced, tears springing to her eyes. "I don't know! My cousin said he had grown up in a haunted house, I had to bring him in because she offered. I couldn't say no! Why what's wrong?"

"He did more than grow up in a haunted house," Dorothy said angrily, turning away. "He knows about iron. He knows how to use it."

"What about iron?" Amy asked. "I don't understand."

"Iron stops us," Dorothy said. She looked back at Amy. "For the weak ones, they are wounded. Too weak to move forward and attack. The stronger we are, the quicker we recuperate."

"And if you were hit with iron?" Amy asked fearfully.

Dorothy smiled grimly. "A few minutes, perhaps more. Still, it is not a pleasant experience."

"What are you going to do?" Amy asked.

"About the intrepid Mr. Ryan?" Dorothy said.

Amy nodded.

"I'm going to kill him," Dorothy replied. "And not quickly, either. I will drag him down to the water's edge and drown him by inches."

Amy smiled and whispered, "I would like that."

Dorothy looked at her approvingly and left the lighthouse.

Amy watched her great-grandmother go and wished she could watch Shane die.

Chapter 59: A Change in Plans

Since there was no bad weather on deck and no heavy fog for the dawn, Al didn't feel any particular pressure in getting the patrol boat out to Squirrel Island faster than he needed to.

Zucci was at the helm, and the rest of the boat's crew went about their work. Harper and Kaplan sat below deck, more than likely arguing about who the Patriots were going to have start the season for defense Al scratched his right forearm compulsively, irritated he had forgotten his nicotine patches at home.

I need to keep some in my locker, he thought.

A sharp flare, bright red, launched up into the sky. It reached its peak and slowly arched.

"Chief, did you see that?" Zucci called back to him.

"Aye, Zucci," Al said, getting to his feet. "Adjust your course, get the men on their lights."

The call went out over the communication system, and men and women scrambled to their lights. Sharp, powerful lights exploded from the helm, the beams crisscrossing the waves and the dark water.

"Strobe to starboard!" someone yelled.

All of the lights swiveled on their mounts, picked through the water and across the white-caps. A yellow life-raft could be spotted, with what looked to be a single person in it. The lights settled on the raft, and the occupant waved their arms.

After several minutes, the boat was as close as it dared to get to the raft. The rescue team was over the side in a matter of moments, and shortly after that, they were back aboard, along with the raft's sole occupant. A young woman, barren of makeup and looking exhausted.

She smiled wearily, tears in her eyes. "Thank you."

Gwen Ouellette, the boat's paramedic, came forward and did a quick, cursory exam as a rescue blanket was wrapped around the young woman.

"She's good, Chief," Gwen said. "We'll have to bring her to the hospital for a full checkup when we get in, though."

Al nodded and stepped forward, dropping down into a squat next to the seated woman. "Hello, miss, I'm Chief Petty Officer Al Arsenault. Can you tell me how you got out here?"

In straightforward, clear sentences the young woman, Courtney DeSantis, told him about what happened to the people who had been aboard the yacht, *A Father's Dream*. She told him about a man trapped on Squirrel Island and the woman named Amy who was there to kill him.

Al stood up, a cold feeling in his stomach. Those who had been around Courtney looked at him.

"Zucci," Al said.

"Chief?" the man asked.

"All ahead, full speed to Squirrel Island," Al said. "Get someone on the horn to base, have them call this in to the city's police. We'll do what we can when we get there."

"Aye aye, Chief," Zucci said.

Al walked over to the stairs and called down, "Kaplan!"

"Aye, Chief!"

"Open the weapons locker."

Al could feel the eyes of the crew on him, but he ignored them and turned his attention back to Squirrel Island.

Chapter 60: On the Road

Marie drove a little over the speed limit, not wanting to have to stop and explain to a State Trooper why she was in a rush.

Or why I think I'm in a rush, she corrected herself. She didn't know for a fact if either Amy or Shane were in trouble. The coincidence was a little too much for her, though.

A missing yacht. A missing gatekeeper at a marina. No word from Amy. Silence from Shane, Marie thought. She checked her mirrors, signaled left, and went around a minivan.

Are you overreacting? she asked herself. *Are you worried something has happened to them? Are you worried they've made a love connection?*

Marie shook her head, chuckling. *No, that's definitely not it. More power to them. I doubt either of them is looking for more than a good time.*

With the travel lane free of the troublesome minivan, Marie got back into it.

It's likely nothing more than Amy having a night on the town, she thought. *How many times has she forgotten her phone at home? Or even forgot to charge it? Or just plain turned it off when she's been having a little too much fun?*

Amy was wilder than Marie would ever be, and she still couldn't understand how the woman did it.

Like all good cops, Marie had a scanner in her car. It was a necessity to her as much as an iPod was to the younger generation. She had the scanner turned down, but loud enough for her to hear. Occasional calls went out. Mostly the mundane, everyday chores of any police force. Moving violations. A rare report of a fight. A domestic assault call and the fear that goes with it.

The scanner squawked as she neared the coast. Some unknown dispatcher at a Maine State Police barracks called out, "We have the Coast Guard reporting a possible 207 at Squirrel Island. I say again, the

Coast Guard is reporting a possible 207 at Squirrel Island."

Marie stiffened as she drove. Her foot suddenly grew heavier, and the accelerator went down accordingly.

207A, she thought numbly. *Possible kidnapping.*

Marie no longer worried about the speed limit.

Chapter 61: Changing Tides

Amy, from her position in the lighthouse looking out the doorway, had seen the flare go up. And she had seen the lights from, what was more than likely, a Coast Guard patrol boat searching the ocean.

She hadn't worried about the rest. All of her great-grandmother's plans were unraveling.

He has to be stopped, she told herself, her thoughts ricocheting madly about her head. *She won't be able to do it alone. Not with the Coast Guard coming. Something has to be done. I have to help.*

After a great deal of struggling and wrenching of her muscles, Amy managed to get her knees up to her chest and her hands under her feet. With her hands in front of her, she was able to find a shard of the broken lantern and cut her bonds.

Amy looked around the scattered tools left by the deceased Mike Puller, and she found a heavy pry bar. The dull blue metal was scratched and pitted, the hooked end of it sharpened to a fair edge.

Good enough, she thought, *to remove Shane's head!*

Clutching the tool tightly in her sore and throbbing hands, Amy made her way out of the lighthouse. She looked around and listened.

From the keeper's house came the sound of something breaking. As though boxes were being broken into.

The children! she thought frantically. *He's in the cellar! He's trying to find the children. If he gets the bodies, she won't be able to bind them here. If she can't bind them, then all of it will have been for nothing!*

Everything will be done.

Shaking with rage, Amy crept along to the keeper's house and made her way to the cellar. In spite of her trembling arms, the pry bar was steady in her hands.

Chapter 62: With the Children

Shane wanted to weep.

The remains of Dorothy's children were pitifully small. He had found a folded tarp near the stairs, and he had spread it out. The last bones, those of the baby, were put with its siblings.

"Why are you sad?" Jillian asked softly.

"I am sad you're dead," Shane answered, keeping a tight rein on his tears. He brought the ends of the tarp together, picked it up, and found the load to be terribly light.

"You don't have to be," Jillian said.

Shane didn't reply as he carried the children up the narrow stairs and into the starlight. He brought them out several feet into the yard and set them down. The wind shifted and carried with it the stink of the bodies in the shed.

Christ, he thought, *I'd forgotten about that smell.*

"I've had enough of you, Shane Ryan!" a woman said.

Shane turned and saw Dorothy. She stood off to the right, far more solid than she had been before.

"Fair enough," Shane replied. "I'm sick of you as well."

"Alas," she said, smiling wickedly, "there is nothing you can do about it."

"Says you," Shane said. He cleared his throat, spat to one side. "You look strong tonight."

"Stronger than I have ever been," Dorothy sneered. "See who I have around me."

She gestured, and the dead appeared around her in all of their horrific glory.

Scott and Dane, Eileen and George. Clark and the boy, Ewan. Jillian, holding a baby, and her grandfather standing beside her. And more. Perhaps another twenty or twenty-five.

Shane didn't bother to count them all.

They'll either side with me, or they won't, he thought.

Shane was armed only with the knuckledusters, having left the makeshift gauntlet and cudgel in the cellar. He took a single step forward and looked to Clark.

"Why are you looking to my husband, Shane Ryan?" Dorothy asked, laughing. "He is my creature. They are all my creatures, bound to me for eternity."

Jillian looked at her mother and walked over to stand behind Shane.

And her grandfather.

And Clark.

Ewan and others followed. The more who left her side, the fainter she became.

Dorothy's face grew cold and harsh.

"This means nothing," she snarled, left only with the newest of the dead, the naked Mike Puller and others beside her. Those too weak to break her hold on them. "I'm still here. And so are they. They'll regret this night, mind you, and I will kill you slowly, Shane Ryan. As slow as I can."

"In the darkness, Dorothy?" Shane whispered.

Her eyes widened, and her face paled.

"No," he said, his voice growing louder. "You'll do nothing in the darkness. But those you murdered will."

"And what will they do?" she asked, a tremor in her voice. One she tried to hide beneath bravado.

"They will give me the strength they deny you," Shane answered.

He crossed the short distance between them quickly.

Mike Puller stepped back nervously, as did the others.

"Do your worst," Dorothy hissed. "I've felt the sting of iron before, and it is no worse than that of a bee."

"Not yet," Shane said softly as if speaking to a lover. "Oh, not yet, Dorothy."

Behind him, he heard Jillian speak.

"We give this to you," the girl whispered.

Terror and pain, violent fear, all of it ripped through him. All of the horror Dorothy had visited upon her victims. The decades of living a nightmare denied salvation or damnation, pummeled Shane.

He grunted, remained on his feet, and absorbed all of it. Every shred of their experiences. It felt as though his blood burned in his veins, as if his lungs would explode, as though the bones would shatter. Shane tilted his head back and screamed, a long, drawn out sound which threatened to drown out the ocean's great voice.

And then it changed.

The scream became a gasp, the gasp a laugh, the laugh a shout of triumph.

Dorothy stood in front of him, as real as the island beneath his feet.

"No," she hissed, looking at her hands. "This cannot be. What have you done?!"

She remained silent as he lunged forward, grabbed hold of her, and dug his fingers into her flesh. She let out a shriek as the fingers pushed through the dress, through the skin, pierced the muscles and gripped them.

With a howl of savage glee, he ripped his hand back, tattering the muscles.

Dorothy tried to jerk away, but Shane didn't let her. He wrapped his hands around her neck and squeezed.

She batted at his arms, grabbed a hold of one of his pinkies and pulled it back, the bone snapping loudly.

Shane bit back a scream, the pain immediate and intense. Stars exploded around the corners of his vision and she wrenched herself away from him. She looked for a way out, but the dead who had sided with Shane made a circle around them. The ghosts kept the two of them contained.

When Dorothy saw she had no escape, she let out a shriek of pure rage and threw herself at him, parts of her arm flapping grotesquely. Shane caught her, grunted at the effort to keep his balance and punched her solidly with his good hand. Something crumpled beneath the blow.

Dorothy's fingers clawed at his face, a thumb catching his lip and slipping into his mouth. The vile taste of her curious flesh made him gag even as she tried to rip his cheek away from his skull.

Shane jerked his head back, threw his fist against her head again and watched as her entire jaw slid to the right. She stumbled and he caught her by the hair, jerking her head back.

Her throat was exposed and as she struck at him, each blow feebler than the last, Shane leaned forward, brought his hand up and began to dig his fingers into her neck.

Chapter 63: Disbelief and Rage

Amy had observed everything which took place between her great-grandmother and Shane. The permanently bald man had looked as though he would collapse, and then the unthinkable had happened.

Dorothy had taken on some sort of physical form.

Shane's obvious scream of pain, and the way he had collapsed, had thrilled her. It had looked like he would succumb to whatever power Dorothy exerted. And then he hadn't.

His screams of pain had become triumphant exultations.

And he had forced, somehow *forced* Dorothy to become real.

There, but not quite.

Exhilaration had filled Amy, and she had tightened her grip on the pry bar. Excitement raced through her as she prepared to watch her great-grandmother destroy Shane.

Yet the opposite had occurred.

Shane had attacked Dorothy. Had literally begun to rip her to shreds. Great chunks of the woman had been cast aside. Those few ghosts who had remained by her great-grandmother's side had fled while those who had betrayed the woman remained behind Shane. All of them pulsed with some strange glow. Their hollow voices rose up in cheers and taunts. They called for Shane, encouraged him, and made certain Dorothy could not escape. Some pushed and kicked at her, and the air vibrated with their excitement.

When Shane bent Dorothy back and tore at the flesh of her neck, Amy froze with horror.

Numb, she watched as Shane let out a howl and he wrenched up with both hands.

Amy's great-grandmother vanished completely.

With a silent rage Amy was spurred to action.

Raising the pry-bar above her, Amy ran forward and brought the sharpened end down, stumbling at the last moment. She slammed the tool into Shane's right shoulder, knocking him forward.

Chapter 64: Gunshots in the Night

When Dorothy vanished, a collective sigh reached Shane's ears. A second later, a terrible pain blossomed in his shoulder.

Shane staggered forward, stumbled and fell. He twisted as he landed and looked up. Through the windows of the keeper's house, and around the sides, a light flashed. A curiously bright illumination. *What the hell was that?* he wondered numbly.

Then he saw her.

Amy had gotten free, and she held some sort of tool in her hand, the top of which was wet.

That's my blood, Shane realized.

She charged at him, and he rolled to one side, lashing out with a foot. He missed her leg as she missed his head.

He managed to get to a knee, and then tried to push off the ground with his right hand. His wounded shoulder wouldn't bear the weight. With a grimace, he slipped down, and he saw her raise the tool up for another attack.

I'll have to meet it head on, he thought dully.

A semi-automatic pistol barked three times, muzzle flashes coming from the left.

Amy stiffened, took a step towards him as someone emptied the rest of the magazine into her.

She collapsed lifelessly to the ground beside him.

Shane looked at her body and thought, *Thank Christ.*

And then passed out.

Chapter 65: At the Dock

Marie made it to the Coast Guard's dock only a few minutes after their patrol boat had docked. Chatter on the scanner had talked about a shooting on Squirrel Island, about a wounded male victim and a dead female assailant. The State Police were sending a boat out to process the crime scene. The Coast Guard was bringing the victim in to be transported to the hospital.

Marie pulled her car in beside an ambulance. All of the vehicle's lights were on, the paramedics in the back.

She had put the car into park, left the keys in the ignition, and hurried to look in the ambulance. Both paramedics were in the back, as was a young woman. The young woman was holding Shane Ryan's hand. He was sitting up on the gurney, shirtless, dirty, and bloodied. When he saw Marie, he nodded.

The paramedics glanced over, and one of them said, "We can't fit any more in here, ma'am."

Marie showed the man her badge and the paramedic shrugged.

"Are you okay?" Marie asked.

"Yeah," Shane said. "They just started a morphine drip for the pain. I'll be useless in about two minutes."

"What happened?" Marie said, glancing at the girl.

Shane shook his head. "Later."

Marie nodded. "Meet you at the hospital?"

"Sure," Shane said, closing his eyes.

Marie turned to leave but stopped as Shane called out, "Hey, Marie."

"Yeah?" she said, looking back at him.

"I will tell you one thing," he said.

"What's that?" she asked.

"No more favors for your family."

Before Marie could ask him what he meant, the paramedics closed the door and the ambulance's engine roared to life.

Chapter 66: Back on the Island

Shane stepped onto the pier and winced. The injuries from his fight with Dorothy were still fresh, only days old. He glanced back at the boat they had chartered and saw Courtney. She stood off to one side with her arms crossed over her chest. Shane knew she had a small piece of iron hidden in her hand. The pilot of the small boat leaned back in his seat, yawned, and checked his phone.

Shane waved to Courtney and she smiled nervously as she returned the wave.

Sighing, Shane turned back to face the island, and started walking along the pier. By the time he reached the path up to the buildings, he could feel the dead gather around him. The air was cold, his exhalations a soft white cloud. He ignored both the lighthouse and the keeper's house, walking around to the back. The door to the shed where he had stored the bodies of Courtney's friends leaned haphazardly, the entire structure leering at him.

A shiver rippled through him, the air growing painfully cold around him as he came to a stop in the spot where he had destroyed Dorothy. The earth beneath his feet felt wrong, the grass a corrupted yellow stain amongst the vibrant green of the rest of the yard.

"Hello," Shane said.

The air around him twisted, folded in on itself and opened and closed, and Ewan had stepped forward. Jillian was with him, the strangulation marks on her neck a vivid red in spite of her translucent nature. The boy had his pipe in his mouth, a wry smile on his lips.

"So," Ewan said, "you've gone and done in Dorothy."

"With your help," Shane said. "I couldn't have done anything without it. Without all of you."

"Right and true," the boy said, "but you were the one who faced her down in the end."

"Thank you," Jillian said softly, looking at him shyly.

"You're welcome," Shane said. He looked from Jillian to Ewan then said, "Will you all be well now?"

"As well as the dead can be," Ewan said seriously.

"I can help you move on, if you wish it," Shane said.

Jillian's eyes widened hopefully, but Ewan's didn't.

"I, myself," Ewan said, "am quite pleased to be here. To look out at the Atlantic, to drift through whatever life this is. There will be others though who might wish it."

Jillian nodded. "I know I do, as well as my siblings."

Shane looked at the tarp where the remains of the Noyes children were tucked away near the house.

He looked from Ewan to Jillian and said, "Thank you, Jillian, for your help."

The girl blushed and for a moment her form lost some of its opaqueness. "I, thank you, Shane Ryan, my siblings and I would like to see what is beyond this island."

"I hope you shall," Shane said. "Good-bye."

The two children said farewell and vanished.

Shane walked over to the tarp, picked it up and carefully carried it away from the house. He set the package down, pulled back the canvas and looked at the remains and swallowed dryly. From the pockets of his cargo pants he took a small bag of salt, a bottle of lighter fluid, and a book of matches. He scattered the salt over all of the bones, then doused them with the flammable liquid. When he finished, Shane stood up, lit a match, and dropped it onto the remains.

The result was instantaneous. A curious, light blue flame arced up to the sky. The fire was smokeless and burned quickly. Soon, nothing remained except ashes.

For a few minutes, Shane stood still, then he pinched the bridge of his nose, wiped his eyes and left the backyard. Long strides returned him to the pier, and then to the boat.

The pilot looked up disinterestedly from his phone and raised an eyebrow. At Shane's nod, the young man put the phone away and started up the boat.

Courtney reached out and took Shane's hand, gently pulling him down to sit beside her. She asked softly, "How did it go?"

"Well enough," Shane replied. "They make me sad."

She nodded, then said, "What now?"

"Now, we go home," Shane said. "Which reminds me, where do you live?"

Courtney grinned. "I live in Manchester, over on the west side. A few minutes from St. Anselm College."

Her grin slipped away and a nervous smile replaced it. "Do you think you might want to get together, maybe have dinner with me?"

"I'd love to," Shane said, squeezing her hand.

The pilot backed the boat away from the pier and headed to port, the lighthouse a silent sentinel. Shane looked at it for a moment, until he saw Clark Noyes standing and watching.

Shane turned his head away from Squirrel Island and looked to the mainland.

Chapter 67: Coffee with Uncle Gerry

"How are you holding up?" Uncle Gerry asked, looking over the top of his coffee mug at her.

"Alright," Marie said. She picked at a thread on the old sweater she wore.

Her uncle looked at her doubtfully.

Marie sighed. "I'm upset."

"About your cousin?" he asked.

She nodded. "The fact that she was responsible for so many deaths, and she nearly killed Shane."

"And how is the young Marine?" Uncle Gerry asked, dropping a hand down to pet the top of Turk's head.

"One," Marie said, grinning tiredly, "he's not young. He's in his forties."

"Still young to me."

Marie shook her head and chuckled. "Two, he's okay. Healing."

"Will you be seeing him later on?" Uncle Gerry said. "Perhaps for dinner?"

"No," Marie replied. "I won't."

Her uncle frowned.

"There's nothing between us, my dear uncle," Marie said. "And, to be perfectly honest, I'm more than happy on my own. I've got a good routine. A good life."

"He's a good man," Uncle Gerry said.

"Without a doubt," Marie responded. "But I don't want a relationship with him, and he doesn't want one with me. Sure, we're friends and I value his friendship, but it won't move beyond that. He's, well, he's got too much baggage, Uncle Gerry. He's too damaged for me. If I'm going to have a relationship, the person has to be okay with who they are. They need to have made peace with their past. Shane is almost happy with who he is, but he certainly hasn't been able to put the past behind him."

"I'm not saying he has to, or that he even should," she continued. "I'm just saying he isn't what I'm looking for in a partner."

Uncle Gerry put his coffee mug down and looked at her silently for a moment. Finally, he said, "What you're saying makes sense. And it's a mature view. I do have one question."

"What's that?" she asked.

"Can I still be friends with him?"

Marie let out a surprised laugh, Turk's ears perking up at the sound.

"Yes," she said, smiling at her uncle, "of course you can!"

"Excellent," Uncle Gerry said, grinning. "Now, tell me about the case you're working on, the one about the body found behind the Holocaust Memorial downtown."

Marie picked up her own coffee, took a sip, and started to give him the gruesome details.

* * *

Bonus Scene Chapter 1: Aboard *The Thin* Man, October 4th, 1893

Ewan McGuire was thirteen years old, though he looked younger, and he had been at sea for nearly two years. As the ship's boy, aboard *The Thin Man* out of Norwich, Connecticut, he had plied the waters along the east coast of the United States. He was a fair hand at many tasks and knew all of the ship's workings by heart.

On the morning of October fourth, he woke when Cookie called him to start the fire for the stove. The men would want their breakfast, and soon. Cookie was the new cook, a green hand from Hartford, a man who clung to the tiny shelves of his kitchen in the meekest of swells.

But he's a fair cook, Ewan thought, yawning. *And he feeds you day and night. He'll get his sea legs soon enough.*

Ewan left the comfort of his small hammock, tugged on his boots and dragged his feet into the galley.

"Good morning, Ewan," Cookie said, his words pronounced with the tight crispness of a New Englander.

"It is," Ewan said, yawning again.

"What's in the skillet?" Ewan asked as he prepped the stove. He laid in some coals, got the fire started and glanced over at Cookie.

"Potatoes and onions, a bit of bacon, and a couple of the smaller apples," Cookie said.

Ewan's stomach rumbled at the idea, and Cookie chuckled. The man pushed his gold-rimmed spectacles back up the bridge of his long nose and set the coffee to boil on the stove top.

Once Ewan had the fire lit, he sat back, took out his pipe and tobacco pouch, and started to fill the bowl. Cookie frowned at him.

"You shouldn't smoke," Cookie said shortly. "It's a bad habit."

Ewan looked over the bowl at Cookie as he lit the tobacco. He drew in several times, stopping once a healthy cloud of smoke curled up from both the briar and his mouth.

"Cookie," Ewan said, "I enjoy your company, my friend, truly I do, but let's not try and squelch the relief I gain from my tobacco."

"It's not relief," the cook said sharply. "It's an addiction. Best to cure yourself of it before you cannot."

"I'll take my chances," Ewan said.

Cookie sucked his teeth at him and shook his head. Several minutes of silence passed as the man went about the galley. He gathered the different items he needed, leaning against the counter as he diced first the potatoes and then the apples.

The ship rolled suddenly, too far to starboard than she had been and Cookie cast a nervous glance at Ewan.

Ewan nodded. "The ocean's a bit heavier than she was. Do you need any more here, Cookie?"

"No," Cookie replied, his voice tight. "Um, what should I do, Ewan?"

"See the bar runs round the top of the galley?" Ewan asked, gesturing with his pipe.

"Yes," Cookie answered.

"There's a length of rope in the locker there. Loop her round your waist, then the other end round the bar," Ewan said. "It'll help to keep you steady. Do you have your knife?"

Cookie shook his head.

"Put it on," Ewan advised.

Cookie frowned. "Why?"

"You may need to cut yourself free right quick," Ewan said. "Best not to be tied to the ship should she go down."

Cookie's face paled noticeably, and with fumbling hands, he reached up to the shelf above the stove. The man took down the leather-sheathed knife Ewan had given him.

"I'll be back as soon as is allowed, Cookie," Ewan said, drawing long on his pipe and exhaling slowly. "I have to see to the Captain."

Without waiting for a response from the cook, Ewan left the galley, scrambling up the stairs and onto the deck. The clouds were a dark gray, the waves growing taller as he made his way to the helm. A few of the hands in the cross-trees, reefing the sails.

Captain Steiner had the helm to himself, the tall, thin man an imposing figure. He had one good eye, the other a milky globe in a field of pale scar tissue. Rumor said the captain had lost it while he was whaling as a young harpooner out of Nantucket. Ewan knew the truth, though. The captain was a killer, having lost the eye in a brutal fight in Prussia at the end of their war with France.

"Ewan," Captain Steiner said, his voice carrying with it only the slightest hint of an accent. "We've a rough sea and worse weather is coming, yes?"

"Aye, sir," Ewan said.

"Scour the deck, boy," the man said, grimacing as he strained against the wheel. "Make sure all is battened down as it should be. Once you're certain, slip away below decks and help Cookie square away the galley."

"Aye, sir," Ewan said.

The waves increased in size as Ewan hurried back to the main deck. He quickly checked lines and belaying pins, stayed out of the way of the men who sailed before the mast and the ship's officers. It was all hands, and each was busy about a task which could mean death for the crew if not done properly. Ewan's eyes were merely another set, one more pair to make certain no little item was missed.

When he was satisfied that he could inspect nothing more, and positive he would be more hindrance than help on the main deck, Ewan went back to the galley.

Cookie was struggling valiantly to get breakfast ready. And he had forgotten to secure his area. Pots and pans were rattling around. Tin cups and plates jangled against one another, spilling out onto the deck as a cabinet door swung open and struck Cookie in the back.

"Oh Hell!" the man said in exasperation, and Ewan felt his own eyes widen.

"Cookie," Ewan said playfully, "my tender ears."

Cookie jerked around, his face flushed with embarrassment.

"I'm sorry, Ewan," Cookie said, stuttering.

"No worries, you know," Ewan said, laughing as he bent down. Quickly, he picked up the spilled dishes and put them away, locking the cabinet tightly. He adjusted the pots and pans and then locked their door as well. With long practiced motions, he fixed the coffee pot to the stove, and the frying pan Cookie was using as well. Ewan went over to the water barrel and saw it was nearly full. He put a bucket beside it and latched the handle of it to a beam.

Cookie looked confused.

"For the fire," Ewan said. "Should we need to douse the coals. Better to drink cold coffee than abandon a burning ship, don't you agree, Cookie?"

Cookie nodded and grabbed hold of the bar over his head as the ship rolled heavily to port. He looked at Ewan and asked, "When will it end?"

"End?" Ewan said. "Good Lord, Cookie. She hasn't even started yet."

Bonus Scene Chapter 2: The Storm

Unfortunately for Cookie, the storm grew worse.

The captain and Hawkins, the first mate, stayed topside through the worst of it, as did Thomason, the second mate. The other crewmen hunkered down below deck to wait out the storm.

Ewan stayed with Cookie, who was violently ill more than once.

After the cook had thrown up for a third time, he smiled weakly at Ewan. As Cookie wiped his mouth with a pocket-square, Ewan asked, "Have you any more left in you?"

Cookie shook his head. "Doesn't mean a thing, though, Ewan. My body will continue to expel whether there is anything left to expel or not."

"I'm truly sorry, I am, Cookie," Ewan said. He relaxed as best he could as the ship continued to roll. His stomach dropped as *The Thin Man* reached the crest of a wave and plummeted down.

Cookie closed his eyes tightly, gasping.

The ship leveled out with a sharp crack and slowly began her ascent once more.

"Ewan," Cookie whispered, "I'd have you know my Christian name in case I drown in this Godforsaken ocean."

Ewan resisted the urge to joke at the man's expense. "Aye, go ahead."

Cookie opened his eyes and said, "My name's Devon Williams. I was chased out of Hartford for, well, things a man shouldn't do."

"Well and good," Ewan said, patting the man on the leg. "You've made a clean breast of it, as far as I can see, so you've no fear now, have you?"

Cookie shook his head. He winced as the ship shifted again and said, "How did you get here, Ewan?"

"Me?" Ewan asked, surprised.

The man nodded.

"Easily enough," Ewan said. "My father and I left Galway three years ago and settled in Nashua. There was work at the mills, then my father, he was killed when they broke up a strike. I was sent to a home, for a bit, run by the Protestants. They tried to break me of the faith, so I left. Made it down to Boston, and Captain Steiner took me as the ship's boy."

"That's a sad story, Ewan," Cookie said.

Ewan shrugged. "Happier than some. The Captain ensures I suffer no abuse. I see the priest whenever we make port, and I am fed and well-clothed. My life is fair, Cookie."

"Do you not miss your parents?" Cookie asked.

"Sure enough, I do," Ewan said. "I smoke my father's pipe, and he always said I had my mother's eyes. They're with God, so I cannot be too sad."

"Don't you wish you had a home, though?" Cookie said. "A place to call your own?"

Ewan laughed. "You know, some of the women at Saint Catherine's have asked the same of me. *The Thin Man* is my home, Cookie. And there, that hammock is a place I call my own."

The ship pitched forward, someone yelled, and Cookie leaned forward dry heaving.

Ewan shook his head at the man's suffering and readied a fresh pipe for himself.

Bonus Scene Chapter 3: The Afternoon

The storm was violent but short. By two in the afternoon, the rough weather was gone, and the seas were as calm as they had been before. Captain Steiner and the first mate's deft handling of *The Thin Man* had brought them through unharmed and the ship wet from stem to stern. But nothing worse.

The same could not be said for the ship they saw on the windward side of Squirrel Island. She was a barque, like *The Thin Man*, and her masts were gone. The tattered remains of one of her jibs still hung from her lines, but the rest of the sails were in tatters. The ship listed heavily to port, and there wasn't any sign of a crew about her.

Captain Steiner called for his glass and when Ewan brought it to him, the man took it out of its leather case and searched for the name.

"Hells bells," the captain muttered, closing the glass and handing it back to Ewan to put away.

"What is it, Captain?" Hawkins asked.

"It's *The Queen's Fist*, out of Bar Harbor," Steiner replied.

"Hamilton's ship," Hawkins said, looking out at the vessel worriedly.

"He's a right smart sailor," Steiner said to Hawkins. "I'm sure he's fine, yes?"

Hawkins nodded and walked away.

"Captain?" Thomason asked.

"They served together," Steiner explained, "in the Federal Navy during the War of the Rebellion. They are good friends. He is worried for him."

"None of the jolly boats are at their davits, Captain," Ewan said, looking hard at the ship.

"Aye, Ewan," the captain said. "Perhaps they went round to the pier. Helm, bring us to the pier, let's see if we can't lend a hand to the crew of *The Queen's Fist*."

As the men went about the process of tacking the sails and the helm

193

adjusted course, Ewan stared at the stricken ship. She looked forlorn and sick, a great water beast waiting for death. The sight of it chilled him and reminded him of the closeness of death on the ocean.

The Thin Man curved around the island, the lighthouse standing tall against the fall sky. No smoke came from the chimney on the keeper's house, and as they came in sight of the pier, they saw a single jolly boat tied up.

"Where are the other two, Captain?" Hawkins asked in a low voice when he returned to stand beside Captain Steiner.

"I don't know, Patrick," the captain replied. "Perhaps they made it into port. I'd hate to think Hamilton abandoned ship so close to land, only to be lost."

"He was a better sailor than that, sir," Hawkins said, frowning. "Much better."

Orders rang out for the anchor to be dropped, and Captain Steiner called for a boat's crew. Hawkins gathered three men to him, as well as the ship's medicine chest.

"Can I go, sir?" Ewan asked, glancing at the lighthouse. "I've not seen the inside of a lighthouse before."

Captain Steiner hesitated, and Ferl, one of the deck hands said, "Squirrel Island is haunted, boy. There's been a sight of killing here, and most of it bad."

Ewan looked at the island and crossed himself. "I'll take my chances, Mr. Ferl, if it is well and good with the Captain for me to do so."

"I'll believe in a Jonah aboard my ship than a ghost on the island, Mr. Ferl," the captain said. "Don't go putting fear into a boy who has none. Ewan, if Mr. Hawkins will have you, then so be it."

"Come aboard and be true Ewan," Hawkins said, smiling tightly. "You've always brought me luck, and I hope you will bring it for me again."

"Aye, sir!" Ewan said happily. Once the jolly boat was in the water, he scrambled over the side and down into the small craft. He was joined a moment later by Hawkins and Julius and Webb, freed men from Louisiana. The men greeted him, shipped the oars, and spoke to one another in their curious patois, none of which Ewan could understand

Within a short time, they pulled in alongside the pier, and Ewan sprang up and out of the jolly boat. Hawkins threw him a line, and he made the boat fast. The men joined him, and all of them stood still.

The island was quiet save for the steady drone of the waves. No gulls called, and no pipers sang.

Julius and Webb spoke quickly in patois. Finally, Julius said in crisp English, "We cannot go farther, Mr. Hawkins. This place, it is no good, do you understand? Webb, he sees what we do not. Hears what we do not. The dead are here, Mr. Hawkins, and they are not pleased. The woman least of all."

Mr. Hawkins nodded. "Stay here with the boat then, though if I shout you need to come running."

Julius and Webb hesitated, then nodded in unison.

"Alright, my stalwart man," Hawkins said, rubbing Ewan's head. "Let's see what can be found here, if anything."

"Aye, sir," Ewan said. He put his pipe in his mouth and followed Mr. Hawkins along the pier. They reached the path and traveled up it towards the keeper's house and the lighthouse.

The doors to both buildings were closed over, and there was no sign of any life.

Ewan felt uncomfortable. As though someone was watching him. He glanced around nervously.

"Do you feel it too, boy?" Hawkins asked softly, slowing his pace.

Ewan nodded.

"Be true," Hawkins said. He veered to the right. When he reached the keeper's house, he put his hand on the door latch, took a deep breath, and pressed down.

The weathered portal opened, and a smell of sickness and death rolled out over them.

"God in heaven!" Hawkins gasped, stepping back. As he did so, Ewan saw into the dimness of the home. Within a heartbeat, his eyes had adjusted, and the scene before him was from a penny dreadful.

All of the furniture in the neatly appointed room was occupied. A pair of young men sat on the settee. An older man sat in a high back chair while two more men sat in Shaker ladder backs. They were arranged around a dining table, the top of which was cluttered with the remains of a meal. Glasses and plates, serving dishes and flatware.

And bones.

Far too many bones.

A giant ribcage from some unknown animal.

"Ewan," Hawkins hissed.

Ewan felt the man reach out, snatch him up, and pull him back.

"They're dead," Ewan whispered as Hawkins reached back and slammed the door closed.

"Aye, lad," Hawkins said, a sickly note in his voice.

"They ate someone," Ewan said, looking at Hawkins. He saw his own horror mirrored in the first mate's eyes. "They ate him. Didn't they?"

Hawkins only nodded in response.

"Why?" Ewan asked. "Why in the name of God would they do that, sir? Why would they eat a man? They weren't marooned!"

"Stand tall, sailor!" Hawkins snapped, holding himself stiffly. "Remember who you are, Ewan!"

Ewan swallowed back his horror and fear, straightened his back, and stood up as tall as he could.

"I don't know what happened," Hawkins said, "or why, for that matter. But I'll need to check the lighthouse. I want you to return to the jolly boat. Stay with Julius and Webb until I return."

"Aye, sir," Ewan said. Part of him wanted to stay with Hawkins. The short distance from the keeper's house to the pier had multiplied by thousands. He could see the two men standing by the jolly boat, watching him and Hawkins.

"Aye, sir," Ewan repeated.

Reluctantly he left Hawkins' side and fought the urge to run.

If I run, he told himself as he walked along the path, *I will look the fool. And what then? The men will laugh that you ran from the dead. What type of sailor will you be then?*

In a short time, he reached the pier, and as he walked along its worn length, he waved to the men.

Julius and Webb returned the gesture, then Webb's eyes widened in fear. He shouted something and Ewan recognized only one word.

"Run!"

Ewan didn't run. Instead, he turned to see what Webb had seen, and he saw nothing.

But as he stood on the pier a bitterly cold wind passed *through* him. It dropped him to his knees and left him shaking, a foul, acrid taste in his mouth. A yell from behind Ewan brought him to his feet, and as he turned around, he saw Julius stumble back, twist around and fall off the pier. The man landed heavily in the jolly boat while Webb chanted in some ancient tongue.

Webb shifted his position as if he were blocking someone from going after Julius. Ewan watched as Webb's head jerked back suddenly, blood exploding from the man's nose. Webb reached up, pulled the old iron cross he wore around his neck from beneath his shirt and ripped it off. With the religious symbol clutched in his hand, he struck out at the unseen force.

A painful shriek caused Ewan to put his hands on his ears. He watched as Webb was lifted and thrown off of the pier as a second, unseen attacker assaulted him. Julius rowed over and then pulled Webb into the jolly boat. Webb took an oar, and they made for the pier again when the entire bow of the craft was jerked down into the water.

Webb dropped his oar, twisted around, and punched the water. The bow sprang up.

"Go!" Hawkins shouted, suddenly standing above Ewan. "Tell the captain!"

Ewan dropped his hands as Hawkins picked him up, threw him over his shoulder and ran back to the lighthouse.

From his bouncing position, Ewan could see Webb grab his oar, adjust it in the lock, and join Julius in rowing madly for *The Thin Man*.

Hawkins reached the lighthouse door, which was opened, and hurtled in. Ewan felt himself roughly dropped to the floor.

The first mate slammed the door closed, and stood behind it, hands resting on the wood. His chest rose and fell as he panted. After long minutes of silence, Hawkins straightened up, turned, and looked at

Ewan.

"Ewan," he said.

"Aye, sir?" Ewan asked.

"Do you still know your prayers?"

"Aye, sir," Ewan replied.

"Best to say them, lad," Hawkins said, taking his hat off and running his hands through his dark brown hair. "I doubt either of us will leave this island alive."

"Why, sir?" Ewan asked, his voice shaking. "Why do you think such a thing?"

Hawkins pointed up.

Ewan lifted his head and followed the line of the first mate's finger.

A man hung from one of the stairs, the hangman's knot done properly.

Ewan crossed himself, looked at Hawkins, and asked, "Is it the keeper?"

The first mate shook his head.

"No lad," Hawkins said sadly, "it's Captain Hamilton, my brother-in-war."

Bonus Scene Chapter 4: In the Lighthouse

Hawkins had cut down the body of his friend and carried it outside. He had covered Hamilton's face with the man's jacket, weighing it down with stones to keep the wind from taking it.

Ewan was glad. He had no desire to see the gulls devouring the soft parts of the man's face.

He and Mr. Hawkins sat in the top of the lighthouse, the lantern dark.

They could see *The Thin Man*. She was still anchored close by. Julius and Webb had reached the ship safely, and the jolly boat was hoisted back aboard. For a while, Ewan had watched the crew scramble about the deck, Captain Steiner occasionally peering at the lighthouse with his glass.

"What do you think they'll do, Mr. Hawkins?" Ewan asked, finally sitting and looking at the first mate.

"Captain Steiner, you mean?" Hawkins asked.

Ewan nodded.

"He'll try and rescue us, of course," Hawkins said, leaning his head back and closing his eyes. "But since it seems we cannot see the ghosts and spirits like Webb can, he will be hard pressed to make any headway."

"But he'll try, sir?" Ewan asked.

"Yes," Hawkins said. "Do not look to hope, though, lad. Webb is a strong man. As is Julius. Both were beaten back by this thing that Webb can see. And let us not forget the scene in the keeper's house. Who knows what drove the men to do what they did? And why are they dead? Did they all take a draught of poison? Was it Hamilton? Did he kill them all before himself?"

Hawkins shook his head. "Far too many questions, my lad. Far too many. I don't think we'll ever have any answers."

The first mate looked as though he might say more, but the sharp, high note of a squeeze-box cut him off.

Hawkins looked at Ewan, and together they got to their feet.

Ewan looked down on the island, walking around the interior of the lighthouse before coming to a stop. In the open area behind the keeper's house were six men. One of them played a squeeze-box quite well. The others moved in a slow, somber dance around him.

And Ewan could see through each of them. They were thin, almost faint sketches as if they weren't truly men at all.

"Sir," Ewan whispered.

Hawkins came and stood beside him. He sighed deeply and said, "Step away, lad. Let's sit down a bit more, shall we?"

Ewan let himself be turned away from the sight. Hawkins sat him down, and then joined him.

"Were they real?" Ewan asked shortly.

Hawkins nodded.

"Dead?"

"Aye, lad," Hawkins replied.

Ewan remembered all the tales of ghosts he had heard in Galway. The stories the men had told at night on the stoops in Nashua.

Stories, Ewan thought. *Nothing more. The old man who liked little boys on the first floor, he was real. And the woman butchered by her brother. She too was real. But ghosts? Never ghosts. Who had to worry about them when there was no food to eat, or when they told you father was dead?*

Ewan looked at Mr. Hawkins. "Are they real, sir?"

"They are," Mr. Hawkins replied. "You don't believe your eyes?"

Ewan shook his head.

The first mate smiled bitterly. "They're often a shock, the first time you see them."

"You've seen ghosts before?" Ewan asked, surprised.

"Aye," Hawkins said, nodding. "Down off the coast of Georgia, during the rebellion. We'd run down a rebel ship, right to ground. The men came streaming out of her though as soon as we came within range to pour in shot. They took to the jolly boats and rowed for us as though the hounds of Hell were after them."

"Were they?" Ewan asked softly.

The first mate shook his head. "No. But it seems they ran aground at an old cemetery. Time and water had ripped at the land, left the graveyard open. I saw a few of the dead. They stood by their headstones and their markers. Whether they meant any harm to Johnny Reb, I know not, but they scared all of us. Hamilton and I pulled a fair few of the southerners out of the water, and then, once we had all we could see, the captain beat to quarters and off we went."

"Did you ever go back?" Ewan asked.

"Would you?"

Ewan shook his head.

Hawkins smiled, got to his feet, and looked out towards *The Thin Man*. The smile faded.

"Looks like the captain's going to try his hand," the man said softly.

Ewan scrambled to his feet and looked out toward the ship.

All of the jolly boats had been lowered away, and in the bow of each, a man held a boat hook at the ready. Those at the oars pulled carefully, the boats moving abreast of each other and keeping a fair course for the pier.

Webb stood in one boat, and when a hidden force tried to pull an oar from a man's hand, Webb lashed out with the boat hook. The oar was freed instantly, and the act emboldened the men. The pace of the boats increased, the oars rising and falling faster. Soon the rescuers had reached the pier and lines were made fast.

"Quick, lad," Hawkins said excitedly, "down the stairs and out the door."

"No," a voice said, and a form materialized. A whisper of a shape against the glass of the lighthouse's lantern. Whatever it was took hold of Mr. Hawkins, and smashed him against the window.

Horrified, Ewan watched as the first mate was lifted off the floor and thrown down. Then the man was picked up and hurled against another window, which cracked beneath the force of the blow.

Hawkins' eyes rolled crazily in their sockets and a tooth hung by a strand of red flesh from his gum. The first mate struggled to get to his feet, but he let out a shriek and collapsed onto his stomach. Blood exploded out of his mouth, and Ewan screamed. A high, piercing sound which broke his voice, leaving him croaking in the lighthouse.

All signs of life fled Mr. Hawkins' eyes, and so too did Ewan flee the top of the lighthouse. His feet started down the stairs, and he tripped, stumbled, and fell towards the stone floor.

Bonus Scene Chapter 5: On Squirrel Island

Captain Michel Steiner was the first onto the pier, a boathook in his hand. He was tense, expecting a cold grip or a sudden blow at any time. His oarsmen came up quickly, equally nervous. After them, came Webb and Julius, Webb speaking rapidly to Julius.

"He sees nothing, Captain," Julius said in a low voice. "He knows they are still here, but they are hiding from him. They know he can see them."

"Well and good, Julius," Michel said, scanning the island with his one good eye. "I am concerned only with Hawkins and the boy. You said they went into the lighthouse, yes?"

"Aye, sir," Julius said.

"Then you and Webb with me, get a boathook for yourself," Michel said. "Let us make short work of this."

Before Julius could reply the sound of a window being broken filled the air. A scream followed, and it was quickly silenced.

Michel ran for the lighthouse. Webb and Julius were with him, as were the others. Their feet thundered on the pier and shook it on its pilings. Michel reached the door first, ripped it open, and stopped short.

The men came up behind him, breathing hard.

"Oh Lord and the man Jesus," Julius whispered.

The boy was dead.

He lay on his back, arms spread wide and legs akimbo. A thin, almost delicate line of blood ran from the corner of the boy's small mouth, along the rise of his pale cheek to drip onto the stone floor. Ewan's soft gray eyes held nothing in them, staring up and seeing a world Michel could not. The boy's briar pipe, the bowl black with use, lay a short distance from the body. Michel stepped into the lighthouse, and a strong hand gripped his arm.

Michel looked back and saw it was Webb who held him. The man spoke softly, and Julius translated.

"Webb says the boy is here," Julius said softly, looking fearfully into the lighthouse.

"His spirit?" Michel asked.

Julius nodded. "He says to leave the body. Take nothing with us from this place."

The thought pained Michel, but he nodded. *I cannot bring the boy's body back with me. Nor anyone's from this place. The crew would never stand for it. Best to report it.*

"Aye, Julius," Michel agreed. "We will take nothing from this place. But I will make sure the boy has his pipe. He loved it over much, but he shall have it still."

Julius translated for Webb, and Webb nodded vigorously. He let go of Michel's arm, and Michel walked into the building. A few steps brought him to Ewan's side, and he crouched down by the boy. Sadly, Michel picked up the pipe and laid it on the child's small chest. With a gentle hand, he went to close Ewan's eyes and sighed thankfully when the lids moved.

So often they do not, Michel thought. He straightened up, turned sharply on his heel, and left the lighthouse.

"Back to the ship, lads," Michel said without looking at his crew. "We're to the dock tonight. I'll report this ere we sail another mile toward New Brunswick."

In silence, Michel led his crew back to *The Thin Man.*

Behind him, in the top of the lighthouse, Captain Michel Steiner felt the ghost of Ewan McGuire watch them go.

* * *

If you enjoyed the book, please leave a review. Your reviews inspire us to continue writing about the world of spooky and untold horrors!

Check out these best-selling books from our talented authors

Ron Ripley (Ghost Stories)
- Berkley Street Series Books 1 – 9
  www.scarestreet.com/berkleyfullseries
- Moving in Series Box Set Books 1 – 6
  www.scarestreet.com/movinginboxfull

A. I. Nasser (Supernatural Suspense)
- Slaughter Series Books 1 – 3 Bonus Edition
  www.scarestreet.com/slaughterseries

David Longhorn (Sci-Fi Horror)
- Nightmare Series: Books 1 – 3
  www.scarestreet.com/nightmarebox
- Nightmare Series: Books 4 – 6
  www.scarestreet.com/nightmare4-6

Sara Clancy (Supernatural Suspense)
- Banshee Series Books 1 – 6
  www.scarestreet.com/banshee1-6

For a complete list of our new releases and best-selling horror books, visit www.scarestreet.com/books

See you in the shadows,
Team Scare Street

Printed in Great Britain
by Amazon